THE WEDDING REJECT TABLE

When Maggie Taylor, a cake decorator, and Chad Robertson, a lawyer from Nashville, meet at a wedding in Cornwall, it's not under the best circumstances. They have both been assigned to 'the reject table' alongside a toxic collection of grumpy great-aunts, bitter divorcées and stuffy organists. Maggie has grown used to being the reject, though when Chad helps her out of a wedding cake disaster she begins to wonder whether the future could hold more for her. But will Chad be strong enough to deal with the other problems in Maggie's life?

ANGELA BRITNELL

◆

THE WEDDING REJECT TABLE

Complete and Unabridged

LINFORD
Leicester

First published in Great Britain in 2015 by
Choc Lit Limited
Surrey

First Linford Edition
published 2018
by arrangement with
Choc Lit Limited
Surrey

A catalogue record for this book is available
from the British Library.

ISBN 978–1–4448–3747–6

Published by
F. A. Thorpe (Publishing)
Anstey, Leicestershire

Set by Words & Graphics Ltd.
Anstey, Leicestershire
Printed and bound in Great Britain by
T. J. International Ltd., Padstow, Cornwall

This book is printed on acid-free paper

Acknowledgements

To June — my wonderful book-loving, wine-loving, life-loving friend. A big thank you to the wonderful Tasting Panel members — Hrund, Linda Sy, Nicky S, Carol N, Betty, Saada, Claire W & Linda Sp — who agreed that the gorgeous Chad was true Choc Lit hero material!

1

Maggie couldn't hold back a heavy sigh as she stared at the wedding reception seating chart.

'Have they stuck you on the RT as well, honey?'

She glanced back over her shoulder and froze. Smiling right at her was the handsome stranger she'd noticed across the aisle in the church. She'd always been a pushover for a man with intriguing eyes and these were tawny, fringed with lashes so long and dark they should have been illegal, and sparkling with good humour. *Stop that right now. You don't do pick-ups at weddings. It's undignified and desperate.*

'What on earth are you talking about?' Her tone of voice was sharper than she'd intended.

'The Reject Table.' His deep smooth voice was laced with a delicious warm drawl she could've listened to all night. 'Of course *they* wouldn't call it that, they might gloss it over by using the term 'Independents', but we know the truth, don't we?'

'Do we?' Maggie bristled. She refused to admit she knew precisely what he was talking about. She'd endured enough of these ritual humiliations while seeming unable to sustain a relationship long enough to change her Facebook status.

'Yeah, sure do. I'm guessin' your English ones are the same as ours. We'll have the elderly maiden aunt, the bitter newly divorced third cousin, the grumpy dishevelled organist,' he counted them all up on his long, well-shaped fingers, 'and of course the mandatory gaggle of single strays.'

'And which category do you fall into?' Maggie couldn't believe she'd asked such a brazen question.

'Take a wild guess,' he challenged, and stepped closer so his arm brushed against hers.

God, he smells delicious. The tempting combination of spicy cologne, soap and something indefinably male wafted in the air and would've made her swoon — if she was the swooning type. Maggie's middle name should've been Sensible.

'Well, you're obviously no one's maiden aunt. The organist was sixty if he was a day and no one could describe you as dishevelled. By the process of elimination I'd say you're the rogue transatlantic cousin representing the groom's American grandmother who's too old to travel.' As soon as he'd spoken it'd clicked in her filing cabinet of a brain. She hadn't helped the bride with the seating plans without gathering some useful information.

'Spot on.' His eyes darkened with surprise. 'How about you?' Maggie winced at his direct question. 'Sorry, sore point?'

She lifted her chin and contrived to look unconcerned. 'Not at all.'

'Forgive me. I'm forgettin' my

manners all around today. I can't believe I said that to a beautiful lady.' He thrust out his right hand. 'I'm Chad Robertson from Nashville in the great state of Tennessee. By day I'm a music attorney, and by night I turn into the rogue you rightly determined me to be. A single one, if you're at all interested.' The almost-question hung in the air between them.

Maggie's curt reply dried in her throat as Chad's strong, warm fingers wrapped around hers in a firm handshake.

'Do you have a name? Fellow single stray.' Chad's warm minty breath caressed the skin on her neck as he leaned down and whispered in her ear.

'Maggie. Maggie Taylor,' she croaked in a distinctly unsexy way. 'Cake decorator and childhood friend of Fiona, the bride.'

'You've got a choice, Miss Maggie, you can eat lukewarm chicken and listen to self-satisfied speeches or sneak away and drink champagne with me in the garden? Which is it to be?' A playful grin crept across Chad's face.

'Won't we be missed?' Maggie said, out of sheer curiosity. She had no intention of giving in to Chad's outrageous suggestion for a multitude of reasons — mainly the fact she was here primarily to work, and the time it had taken to get her oldest friend married off was her only reprieve.

'I sure won't be. Peter barely knows me from Adam and I only met Fiona for the first time yesterday. It might be different for you.' His gleaming eyes swept down over her and every cell in Maggie's body vied for attention. 'I can't imagine not missing you.'

She was stunned into silence.

'I'm game if you are.' Chad offered and Maggie couldn't resist smiling back.

'There you are. I've been looking for you *everywhere*.' Emily's exasperated voice broke through the moment and her sister appeared right by them. 'I need you in the kitchen right now.' She frowned and grabbed hold of Maggie's arm. 'There's a problem with the cake.'

Typical. This was her luck in a nutshell. Good-looking, single man appears and flirts with her and naturally she has to go back to work. 'Don't panic, Ems, it'll be alright,' she reassured and gave Chad an apologetic shrug before turning away. By the time she sorted out the cake her would-be Prince Charming would've found himself another Cinderella.

★   ★   ★

'Sorry to drag you away from the gorgeous hunk you were drooling over,' Emily quipped. 'I'll let you have another go at him as soon as you've worked out what to do with *that*.' She flung open the swinging door into the kitchen and pointed to what had been the bride's dream cake. The elaborate pink and white, five-tiered confection made of luscious almond sponge and layered with fresh raspberries was now

6

strewn all over the table and floor, the wreckage resembling a war zone.

Maggie bit her lip hard enough to draw blood. It was the only way to stop from screaming or bursting into tears, neither of which would help the situation. She and Emily had only formed Two Hearts Catering two months ago and this was their first proper contract — she didn't count providing sausage rolls and cocktail pasties for their Aunt Judy's sixtieth birthday party a couple of weeks ago. Failing today wasn't an option. 'Tell me what happened.'

Emily launched into a long, rambling story involving the obnoxious five-year-old twin boys belonging to the bride's sister, a foot race through the kitchen and a search for buried treasure in the precious wedding cake. It was pointless to ask why no one had stopped them because the damage was done now.

'You need to go and help hand around the canapés,' Maggie said with unnatural calm as she glanced at her watch. 'We've got an hour before the cake has to be in position, although we could stretch it a little if we have to.'

Emily's lip trembled meaning she was on the verge of bursting into tears. To say her older sister used her soft, fragile appearance for her own benefit was an understatement. Men routinely fell at her feet professing undying love, but Emily had found her Prince Charming in the form of her fiancé, Jonathan. Maggie only hoped he wouldn't tire of Emily's unpredictable behaviour. A few times recently she'd heard him snap at her sister about something she'd said or done, and only yesterday she'd caught Jonathan staring hard at Emily when he thought he wasn't being watched.

★　★　★

Giving her credit where it was due Emily's cooking *was* out-of-this-world even if her business sense could fit on the head of a pin. The mantle of responsible, reliable half of the company had naturally landed on Maggie. Right now she could do with a shoulder to cry on herself and she briefly allowed herself to recall Chad Robertson's excellent broad shoulders, the ones framed by his exquisite designer suit.

'But . . . '

'Go and do what you do best, feed people and be nice to them. Let me worry about this.' Maggie cut off Emily's protests and shooed her sister out of the kitchen. She forced herself to ignore the pitying looks being thrown her way by the rest of the catering staff. Taking a couple of slow, deep breaths she tried to settle her churning stomach. Maggie walked over to the sink and washed her hands before putting on an apron to cover up her dark green taffeta dress.

Then she cleared her head and started to think.

2

Chad waited a few minutes but Maggie with the captivating smile, tempting curves and sparkling blue eyes didn't return. Just his luck. If she didn't come back soon he'd be stuck making polite conversation with the other down-on-their-luck souls on the Reject Table. His colleagues and friends in Nashville would laugh themselves silly. The idea that anyone would seat Chad Robertson anywhere but at one of the best tables would amuse them no end. He hadn't been the top prize in the recent Music City Bachelor Auction for nothing, raising $50,000 for the local children's hospital thanks to a bidding war between two of the city's top hostesses.

Top of his agenda was to find out more about the fascinating Maggie. She was the first woman in a long time to stir him from the lethargy he'd sunk into recently — one which made no sense for a red-blooded thirty-year-old man with the world at his feet. He couldn't precisely pinpoint what the attraction was either. The English woman was almost tall enough to look him in the eye but seemed uncomfortable with the fact. Maggie's outdated dress, natural brown hair ruthlessly pinned up in a bun and minimal make-up made her far from the petite, glossy, well-turned out women he usually dated.

Yeah, but what about her clear skin, sparkling eyes and kissable mouth? And the hint of vanilla and spice you sniffed when you got close? Telling himself her delicious scent came from cake baking wasn't doing the trick. He needed to track her down again and soon.

Chad glanced around the expansive entrance hall dominated by a stunning Victorian chandelier and noticed the classic moulded ceiling and the genuine oil paintings dotted around the walls.

He hadn't had the chance to check out the rest of the place yet but the small, country-house hotel was furnished with enough antiques to make his father extremely envious. Although Chad had been to London several times he'd never made it down to Cornwall before. He liked what he'd seen so far and planned to look around some before heading back to Nashville next week.

He made his way into the bar where everyone was congregating for the pre-dinner appetisers while they waited for the bride and groom to finish with the photographer. Apart from his aunt and uncle, Chad only vaguely knew a couple of his English cousins but talking to new people didn't bother him. Most people enjoyed talking about themselves, plus he had the advantage of being a foreigner so would shamelessly turn on his Southern charm.

Chad decided to start with the young, dark-haired waitress carrying around trays of drinks. He gave her the full force of his smile, instantly making her stop by him. Chad selected a glass of white wine, quite certain it would be lukewarm but not willing to risk the red while wearing a pristine white shirt and new grey linen suit. 'So, sweetheart, is the food going to be any good?'

'Absolutely,' she beamed, 'Emily and Maggie are great.'

'Really?' Chad encouraged, and she happily chattered away, going into lengthy details about the two sisters and their new catering company. Maggie was clearly the brains of the business and her sister the creative cook. But wedding cakes were apparently Maggie's real love and the waitress claimed she was the best thing going. Chad smiled to himself. He'd thought she was pretty damn good too although he had to concede cake and icing weren't at the forefront of his mind when he made that summing up. 'I'd better not keep you away from your work any longer.' He apologised with a smile and the girl nodded and hurried off.

Across the room Maggie's sister was

passing around trays of food so Chad inched his way through the crowd until she was within arm's reach. Emily's thin shoulders were rigid with tension and her bubbly smile didn't reach her soft blue eyes. Chad tried to imagine what sort of disaster could befall a wedding cake and failed. *Time to work his magic again.*

'What are those good-looking nibbles, honey?' He laid the Southern drawl on as thick as molasses in winter. Chad pointed at the curious things she was trying to foist on people and received an engaging smile in return.

'They're Scotch eggs. Would you care to try one?'

'Sure. Why not.' *Uh. Maybe because you can see a hard-boiled egg is involved and you hate them worse than okra?*

'We wrap herbed sausage meat around the cooked egg before covering it in breading and then deep fry it. They're very traditional.' Emily explained and Chad forced his smile to

14

remain intact as he selected one from the tray and took a large bite.

It took every ounce of good manners Chad possessed not to spit it right back out. The thing was cold making it even more revolting than he'd expected. 'Interesting,' he managed to say and caught the hint of a genuine smile lurking around Emily's mouth. Now he could see the resemblance to her sister.

'Peter loves them but they're not my favourites either if that's any consolation.' Her dry summing up allowed him to agree.

The sound of a loud gong being rung several times stopped their conversation and Chad listened to the announcement of the bride and groom's arrival. In a few minutes he'd have to find his table with no hope of a reprieve.

'Excuse me. I must go and make sure dinner is ready to serve,' Emily explained.

'Of course.' He couldn't logically keep her there much longer. 'Oh, by the way, did you solve the cake problem?'

She paled under her freckles. 'Maggie promised me everything will be fine. She's never let me down and I'm sure she won't today.'

A lump tightened Chad's throat and he tried to convince himself it was undigested cold sausage rather than unwelcome emotions. He was pretty sure his brother wouldn't make the same observation about him. Being ten years apart they'd never been close as boys, and as adults the combination of geography, lifestyle differences and a lack of effort meant they rarely met these days. When they did see each other there was none of the companionship he'd spotted between the two sisters.

'She strikes me as the kind of girl who'd stick to her word.'

Emily gave him a curious look, blatantly sizing him up. 'Really? Considering you only met her an hour ago I can't imagine how you could possibly know that.'

He was being given the cold English

attitude he'd heard about. How did they do it while still sounding so polite? 'Well, isn't she trustworthy?' He went on the offensive and got a mild kick of pleasure when she nodded. 'By the way I never did introduce myself. I'm Chad Robertson, cousin of the groom. I'd shake your hand but you might drop those delicious eggs.' His tone was teasing but he was happy when Emily managed a slight smile.

'I see why Maggie was annoyed at me dragging her away now.'

A rush of heat flamed up his neck at the pithy comment and for one of the few times in his life Chad found himself speechless.

'Enjoy your meal.' Emily breezed off leaving him standing there with the remains of a Scotch egg in his hand. Making sure no one was looking he deposited it in the nearest plant pot and reluctantly followed everyone into the dining room.

The things he did for his grand-mother.

* ★ ★

Maggie nibbled at her lip and concentrated. If this didn't work Fiona might never speak to her again. She'd cleaned up the floor first — being sued because someone broke their leg slipping on the sticky mess was the last thing they needed. Next she'd salvaged what she could from the remains on the table and retrieved her emergency box of supplies from the car. With a reserved slab of almond cake and a big container of butter cream icing she would do her best. Maggie had forgotten to put in any extra raspberry puree but it was too late to fret over that now. There was no way she could transform this disaster back to the five tier creation she'd spent the last two days working on so it was time to make up a Plan B.

'You haven't done anything!' Emily shrieked and Maggie nearly dropped her knife. 'We'll start taking around the prawn cocktails in another ten minutes. How long do you think I can drag out serving the rest of the meal?' The hysterical edge to her sister's voice didn't do anything for Maggie's confidence.

'Fiona originally wanted a cupcake tower and her mother talked her out of it. But she's the bride so we're going to sort of give her what she really wants,' Maggie explained with as much patience as she could muster, all the while cutting cake and fitting it into paper cases she'd discovered in one of the kitchen cupboards.

'You can't do that. How're you going to explain . . . '

Maggie snorted. 'I'm not going to. You are.'

'Me?'

If Emily wasn't so young and fit Maggie wouldn't have been surprised to see her sister have a fatal heart attack on the spot.

'Yes, you,' Maggie stated firmly. 'People always believe you. They think you're sweet and innocent and never lie.'

Emily's mouth flopped open and closed like a goldfish.

'You'll take Fiona to one side and explain that the cake won't look as she expects because it will be so much better. Tell her we always put the bride's wishes first and we felt she wasn't happy with the original plan.' The explanation tripped off Maggie's tongue and she wondered if she should've gone in for politics instead of cake decorating.

Emily rolled her eyes in horror. 'You're mad.'

'Do you have a better idea?' she challenged, a tiny bit satisfied when her sister shook her head. 'I didn't think so. This is how you're going to describe it.' Maggie ploughed on before she lost her nerve. She'd come up with the brilliant idea of calling the new design 'deconstructed cupcakes' — deconstructed was the new culinary buzz word and she'd do whatever was necessary to get away with this.

'Fine.' Emily sighed. 'When do I have

to humiliate myself?'

Maggie ignored the sarcasm and proceeded to make herself very clear. Nothing was to be said until the main course had been served so there was no time for Fiona to throw a wobbly. 'Now get on with the prawn cocktails and leave me to salvage our reputation.'

Emily swung around on her heels and headed for the other end of the kitchen. After picking up a loaded tray she turned and glanced back at Maggie with a mischievous smile.

'Oh, by the way, I forgot to tell you I spoke to your admirer earlier.'

A fierce rush of heat flooded Maggie's face.

'The hottest single man in the room and you're stuck in the kitchen mending cupcakes. Not fair is it?' Emily breezed out, leaving Maggie to bite back a curse that would've shamed a sailor.

3

Chad gave a swift glance towards the Reject Table at the back of the room and a bleached blonde in a skin-tight red dress met his gaze, shamelessly ogling him. Emily and a tribe of waitresses carrying silver platters emerged from the kitchen and began to circulate. *Time to make a detour.*

He sidled around the edges of the room until he reached the kitchen door and sneaked inside. Chad's gaze homed in on Maggie, bent over a table and completely engrossed in her work. It gave him the opportunity to admire her shapely figure from behind and he swiftly decided he'd been right the first time. Thank goodness he was an observant man because her tempting curves were well-disguised under the hideous green dress. Scarlett O'Hara's curtains would be a distinct improvement.

'How's it goin'?'

She startled at the sound of his voice, dropped a spoon on the floor and jerked around with a fierce glare. 'What on earth are you doing in here?'

Not the warmest welcome he'd ever received from a woman, but Chad sauntered across the room watching Maggie's cheeks flame as he got closer. 'I thought I'd see how you were getting on and whether there was any chance of you coming back out and rescuing me any time soon?'

A tiny smile pulled at her mouth. 'I don't have time to . . . talk.'

Flirt. You were going to say flirt. The charming deep pink colour creeping all the way up your neck says that for you.

He checked out the table behind her, strewn with cake, icing and something red and jelly-like, and let out a long, low whistle. 'What the heck are you goin' to do with that?'

'Turn it into an amazing creation that will be the talk of the wedding,' Maggie declared, defiantly lifting her chin.

'Oh, they'll be talkin' about it alright, honey.'

She pointed her finger at him. 'Get out, now, or . . . '

'Or what?'

'Do something useful.' The challenge in her sapphire eyes uncurled a coil of desire in Chad and he fought to squash it back down. Appearing to be nothing better than a sex-starved, mouthy American wasn't going to win over this straight-talking woman.

Chad shrugged off his coat and hung it on the back of a chair. While she continued to watch he removed his engraved platinum cufflinks and slipped them in his trouser pocket before rolling up the sleeves of his shirt. 'I'm yours. Tell me what to do.'

She stared in complete disbelief and then burst out laughing; a rich warm sound that heated every inch of his skin.

'You're a guest. You're supposed to sit between Tonya, the desperate divorcee, and Fiona's sharp-tongued Great

Aunt Audrey. Charming them and keeping the peace is your job for today.'

He grinned. 'And you know this because?'

'I helped Fiona with the seating plan.'

'But didn't arrange to sit next to me yourself?' Chad lowered his voice and closed the gap between them. Catching a drift of Maggie's unique scent made him want to nibble her neck to see if she tasted as good as she smelled. 'Slipped up there, didn't you?'

I knew exactly what I was doing. She'd told Fiona it was pointless to assign her a seat because she wouldn't have time to use it, but her friend insisted. Maggie wasn't intending on explaining to Mr Tempting about her abysmal record with men. She'd had more dating disasters than the Queen had planted commemorative trees and wasn't ready for another round anytime soon. Maggie allowed her gaze to drift down over him, all smooth, pressed and yummy. She guessed he could lure a woman away from her good intentions with one kiss, but she wasn't planning on finding out.

'I assume Tonya is the blonde vixen waiting to make me her lunch?'

Maggie stifled a giggle and nodded. 'You spotted her?'

'*She* spotted *me* all the way across the room.' Chad rolled his eyes.

'So you decided I was a safer bet?'

The searing look he gave her could have barbecued a steak in three seconds flat. 'Oh, honey, there's *nothing* safe about you.' If he was a cat he'd be purring. Maggie should have found his obvious, in-your-face flirtation hilarious but the grin spreading across his face told her Chad was doing this on purpose. She wasn't sure why, or if she wanted to find out.

'Leave me alone,' she whispered, 'I've got to get this finished.'

'And I've offered to help.' He folded his arms and planted his feet slightly apart making it clear he'd no intention of moving any time soon.

'Fine. Put this on or you'll ruin those pretty clothes.' Maggie tossed him a 'Two Hearts' apron and smiled as he held it up to examine it, not quite managing to hide his dismay. She was proud of the design but had to admit nothing about it was manly. The fine white linen was softened with red lace ruffles and strewn with entwined scarlet hearts along with hers and Emily's initials.

Chad's dark eyebrows rose but he didn't say a word, only slipped the apron on over his head and gingerly stretched the wide red satin belt around his waist before tying it in a loose bow at the back. 'Give me instructions. I'm all yours.'

She bit her tongue on the response that'd randomly popped into her brain — something along the lines of 'I wish you were.' She'd wasted five precious minutes she didn't have and forcibly switched back into work mode. Maggie pointed to the small square cake set over on one side of the table. 'I managed to salvage that and am turning it into a cake for the bride and groom to cut. Everyone else is having my version of a cupcake.' He scrutinised her hard, as if she was explaining how to make an atom bomb instead of a simple cake. 'Just shape whatever cake you can find from the pile into these cases. I'll ice them when you're done.'

'Uh, won't they fall apart when people try to eat them?'

His sharp question hit on the flaw in her plan and she tried to come up with a reasonable reply.

'I don't suppose you have any ice cream cones?' Chad asked.

'I don't know, but that's a brilliant idea.'

He beamed and her stomach did a few heart-stopping somersaults.

'Happy to be of assistance,' he declared and started rifling through cupboards. Maggie followed suit. No luck of course. That would've been too easy and nothing in her life was ever simple. Maggie ran into the store cupboard and stared in vain at the rows of canisters, huge bags of potatoes and industrial sized bottles of ketchup. One of the main reasons Fiona chose to have her reception here at Polvennor House was because she'd had the option of using the usual hotel staff or bringing in her own caterers. Taking over a kitchen for a day was a huge challenge, not the least of which was the fact that Maggie's habit of knowing exactly where everything was didn't apply.

'Eureka!'

She glanced over her shoulder and stared at Chad now grinning like the proverbial Cheshire Cat and waving a jam jar in the air.

'Serving food in small jars is the latest craze in Nashville. All the hip restaurants are taking what we call Mason Jars that are used for canning, and either baking in them or layering the stuff in unique ways. They charge a ridiculous amount and everyone thinks they're cool.'

She hated to put a damper on his

enthusiasm, but being the realistic one was her slot in life. 'That's great, but I doubt they've got a hundred of those things and that's how many I need.'

'Use glass tumblers as well.' He suggested. 'You don't strike me as a givin' up sort of gal. Use your imagination. Part of the supposed charm is that they don't have to all match.'

His challenge hit a nerve. Maggie prided herself on always finding a solution to whatever problem threatened to trip her up. 'I did tell Emily to describe them as deconstructed cupcakes and you can't get much more taken apart than cramming what's left into a glass.'

'Right. How about I try to rustle up enough containers while you get on with the main cake? You can give me instructions when I'm ready.' His smooth drawl sharpened and stopped Maggie in her tracks. Appearances certainly could be deceptive. People would no doubt mark this man down as laid-back and easygoing, but she'd guess that was a million miles from the truth.

'Sounds good. Let's get busy.' She gave him a shy smile. 'Thanks. I'm not sure why you're doing all this for me but for now I'll consider you my guardian angel and leave it at that.'

* * *

For the second time today Chad was struck dumb. No one had ever called him their guardian angel before; his clients used far pithier names if he failed to get the deal they thought they were entitled to. Even his family considered him to be a typical self-serving attorney, while still loving him. So why did smart, funny Maggie think differently of him?

He managed to nod and bent down to pick up the box of jars he'd found. Luckily by the time he stood back up she'd disappeared back into the kitchen. Chad took a few slow, deep breaths and headed back in to get busy. No way was he letting Maggie down.

4

'What's *he* doing?' Emily's shrill voice broke Maggie's concentration. 'Are you so desperate you went out there and dragged him into the kitchen?'

Chad held his breath and mentally counted to ten. If he didn't control his rising temper Miss Emily would be wearing the tub of icing in his hand, and that would be the least of her problems. The back of Maggie's neck turned a violent shade of scarlet and he hadn't felt as sorry for anyone in a very long time.

'*I* came to see Maggie and offered my help, no coercion needed,' Chad explained. And to think he'd envied their apparent closeness earlier.

'Why?'

He raised an eyebrow and put on his best unreadable legal face. 'Why not?' *Always throw a question right back at them*. A mentor told him that at his first internship out of law school and it'd never let him down yet.

'Please get on with serving the main courses, Emily.' Maggie's icy tone sent shivers through Chad, but her sister only snorted and flounced off. Bending her head Maggie clutched at the edge of the table and waves of unadulterated fury shimmered in the air around her. He hurried over and placed his hands on her shoulders, gently easing her around to face him. A film of tears glazed her pretty eyes.

'That was the meanest thing I've heard in a while.' He rubbed a finger slowly down her cheek, briefly registering that her skin was as soft as he'd expected. 'You don't deserve being spoken to that way.'

'How would you know?' A deep vein of sadness ran through her voice and he dropped his hands away. 'I need to get back to work.'

'That's it?'

Maggie stiffened. 'Yes.'

'Fine, if that's the way you want it.'

'It is.' Turning away from him she picked up an icing bag.

For now he'd let her get away with it, but they weren't done discussing what was going on between the two sisters by a long chalk.

★   ★   ★

The swirl of noise and chatter coming from the other end of the kitchen where Emily and the rest of their staff were busy was in complete contrast to the throbbing silence filling the air between her and Chad. She didn't intend to explain herself to a complete stranger, even a handsome one who'd done nothing but be kind to her.

She needed to push everything from her mind apart from the task in hand, but it wasn't easy. Maggie started to smooth out the icing she'd put on the small cake and concentrated on getting the sides right. An earlier dig through the freezer had unearthed a bag of frozen raspberries and she'd shaken them out into a colander to thaw while she worked. Now she dried them off and took her time arranging them around the base of the cake. Luckily when they'd arrived this morning she'd put the flowers for the top in the fridge so they'd escaped the carnage. Maggie sensed Chad's eyes boring through her back as she retrieved the small arrangement of deep pink roses and set it down in the centre before standing back to see how it looked.

'It's beautiful.' His husky words forced her to turn around and look at him.

'Thank you.' Maggie managed a tight smile. 'You're doing well,' she conceded, noticing the long line of cupcake filled glasses in front of him.

'Not sure I'll be giving up the law to start my own bakery anytime soon, but it's always useful to have another talent.' His enigmatic reply was unsettling.

'Yes, well, I'll start icing the ones

you've finished while you carry on with the others.' Chad's intense gaze unnerved her and she dropped the piping bag she was holding. He leapt forward and caught it a second before it could hit the floor.

'Butter fingers,' he teased.

'Butter cream icing actually.' Maggie grinned, unable to keep up her cool attitude any longer.

Chad placed the bag in her out-stretched hand, but before she could whip it away wrapped his long, lean fingers around hers and held on tight. The warmth rising from his tanned skin made her hotter than she'd any right to be. Maggie's gaze slid to the soft dark hairs on his muscular forearm, itching to stroke her fingers down over them.

'Do you know what I think?'

No. Pretty sure I don't want to. She shook her head and waited, nibbling at her lip while he did the staring thing again.

'I think we need to get back to work.'

Maggie exhaled slowly and caught

the hint of a smile lurking in his eyes. He'd done all that on purpose. Chad sauntered away and her shoulders sagged with relief, at least that's what she'd claim if anyone asked. *Are you sure you aren't disappointed because he didn't kiss you?* She refused to answer the naughty voice in her head and went back to work. Dealing with inanimate icing was much safer than this flesh and blood man who appeared to see right through her.

*   *   *

Years of practise at concealing his emotions stood Chad in good stead now. His gut was in tortuous knots but he was sure no one would guess by looking at him. He wasn't *sure* what just happened but suspected he'd fallen hard for Maggie Taylor. While his mind spun around in circles Chad continued to fill jars and glasses, smoothing off the tops before pushing them to one side. Kissing her would've been so easy, but at the last second he'd drawn back. Harmless flirting was part of his easy-going persona, but it wasn't good enough for Maggie. He realised that now.

Chad worked on steadily and steeled himself not to keep glancing over at Maggie who was equally intent on her speed-icing. 'How much longer do we have?' he asked and she frowned up at the large black railway clock on the wall.

'Not long enough. The cake should be in place by now for people to admire. Thankfully Fiona and Peter decided they weren't going to do without pudding after the meal so we've got miniature chocolate cheesecakes and lemon granitas ready to go out next.' Maggie gave him a quizzical look. 'Why are you looking confused? It's not complicated.'

'I'm guessin' it's a language thing. I'm imagining you serving the childish chocolate pudding out of a box that I would've lived on if my Mom let me but I'm guessin' pudding to you is any sort of dessert, right?' Chad ventured.

'Of course.' Her words had a slight edge but the sharpness was mitigated by the hint of pink colouring her cheeks. For the second time in a few short minutes it almost took more willpower than he possessed not to give in to the urge to kiss her.

With a flourish he finished filling the last glass. 'There you go. All done.'

Maggie's eyes shone. 'Wow. You're amazing.'

Chad wished she wasn't talking about his creativeness with smashed cake but for now would take what he could get. 'All part of the service.'

'Would eating lunch with Tonya and Great Aunt Audrey really have been worse than this?'

I'd scrub the damn floor I'm standing on to be in here with you. Of course he didn't dare be that honest. She expected light-hearted and that's what he'd give her. For now. 'Far worse. Between them they'd have eaten me alive.'

'There's still time. Why don't you go out and join them while I finish icing these?'

'Are you rejecting me too?' Chad said with a rueful smile and Maggie opened her mouth to speak but nothing came out but a strangled breath. 'I *really* hope not,' he murmured and stared deep into her eyes. 'You need to get back to icing.'

'Yes.' The reply came out automatically but she didn't move.

The kitchen door slammed back against the wall and Emily ran in. 'You'd better get out here and do something with Fiona. She's furious because there's no cake on display yet and hasn't bought my feeble explanation.'

'I'm sorry but I've got to get this finished. You need to go back out and smooth things over. Usually you don't find pulling the wool over people's eyes a challenge,' Maggie retorted, and Chad held his breath, waiting for the inevitable explosion.

5

What was she thinking? Upsetting Emily was always a bad idea. Maggie had caught on to that as a small child and learned to tiptoe around her sister's volatile temper. The phrase 'mood swings' must've been created with Emily in mind. Their parents explained that Emily was 'sensitive' but Maggie suspected her sister hadn't liked her arrival one bit and behaved badly on purpose. After three years as an adored only child she'd made sure no one would overlook the family's princess.

'You'll pay for this later,' Emily hissed and left in a flurry of temper.

Oh, I know I will.

Maggie caught Chad staring at her with frank curiosity and swallowed hard.

'Do you want me to help you get this display together?' His soft, sympathetic words made her want to throw herself into his arms.

Don't be stupid. Maggie nodded, biting back tears. 'I'll ice the last half a dozen and then we'll start.' She stepped back to her table and tried in vain to ignore Chad's quiet breathing behind her, so close she could've reached back and touched him. Five minutes and she was finished. 'All done.' She turned to face him, plastering on a tight smile.

'What's the plan, or isn't there one?' His mischievous question made Maggie laugh, unable to resist his easy good humour.

'Why would you think I don't have one?'

Chad raised one black straight brow.

'I did have a very detailed plan,' she explained, 'but it needs to be adjusted now.'

'So I'd guessed and don't bother suggesting I leave you to it either. You're not throwing me back to the sharks at the Reject Table without being by my side to protect me.'

43

Maggie tossed her hands up in the air. She'd never met such a persistent man. They must breed them stubborn in Tennessee. And flat out gorgeous. Even a red lacy apron couldn't hide Chad Robertson's easy, graceful masculinity. She'd never met a man before who could make her laugh, think and want to run her hands all over him in equal measure. Maggie was rapidly losing the battle against giving in to him.

'I came across a couple of round mirrors when I was digging out all the glasses earlier. Do you think you could do something with them?'

'Another great idea, Sherlock.'

He dragged his piercing gaze shamelessly down over her and Maggie's body lit up like a Christmas tree. 'You sure don't resemble any Holmes I've ever seen.' His smooth drawl slid over her and made her want to listen to him forever. *Forever? You're losing your marbles.* The effect of rescuing her best ever wedding cake from culinary manslaughter must have affected her brain.

* * *

Chad wasn't being fair to either of them, but couldn't stop himself. Did she realise the effect she was having on him? Somehow he doubted it. Maggie seemed transparent and he suspected that what you saw was what you got. He found that beyond sexy.

'Mirrors?'

He mentally shook himself. 'Yeah, sure.' Chad strode away before he could behave even more stupidly. *Not possible, bro.* Josh's laconic voice ran through his head. A pang of loneliness ran through him for his older brother. When he returned to Nashville maybe he'd reach out to Josh and if the friendly gesture was thrown back in his face at least he'd have tried.

He hadn't wanted to make this trip to Cornwall, but his grandmother insisted and he wasn't brave enough to refuse Rose Ann Robertson. She was too old to travel and his parents had the family's guitar business to take care of so he was dispatched to represent the Robertson side of Peter Carlisle's family. Chad hadn't been able to use the excuse of not being able to take time off work because his grandmother knew he'd wrapped up his latest contract negotiation and been urged by the firm to use the increasing number of vacation days owed to him. He'd made the foolish mistake of asking why Josh wasn't being sent instead and received one of his grandmother's withering glances. Her blunt reply was that Josh 'doesn't own a suit', although they both knew there was far more to it than the lack of appropriate clothes.

Now here he was scrabbling around in the storeroom of a small hotel in the wilds of Cornwall searching for mirrors to make a woman happy. Go figure.

Chad lifted down the mirror he'd spotted earlier and discovered two others on the next shelf. Holding them carefully he returned to the kitchen. 'There you go,' he declared, instantly rewarded by another of Maggie's glorious smiles.

'Perfect.'

Yeah, you're pretty perfect too.

'We'll have to assemble it out there.' Maggie sighed. 'I'll go and move the table into position then you can bring the largest mirror out first.' She grinned. 'You might want to take off the apron before you venture very far.'

He put on a forlorn expression and lifted up the lace ruffle around the hem in pretend admiration. 'I've become quite fond of this.'

'If you're good I'll let you keep it as a souvenir of your first, and I'm guessing last, foray into the catering world.'

There were so many replies he could make on a number of different levels but Chad contented himself with a broad smile. That did the trick because she laughed again and he enjoyed her unfettered pleasure in the moment. He untied the bow, slipped the apron up over his head and shook his hair back into place.

★　★　★

Maggie's heart flipped. She itched to run her fingers through Chad's thick black hair, cut perfectly and gleaming under the florescent lights. If she hadn't restrained her own mass of brown wavy hair in a tight bun this morning it'd be all over the place and already random strands were making a frizzy halo around her face. Before she could make even more of a fool of herself she stalked out of the kitchen, leaving Chad with a bemused expression.

She made her way quietly along behind the guest tables to the back corner of the room and shook out the cloth she was carrying to spread over the circular table. Made of cream-coloured antique lace it had belonged to Fiona's grandmother. Maggie smoothed out the top and made sure it was hanging evenly all around the bottom. Standing back up she caught Emily staring at her from across the room where she was refilling wine-glasses. For a second she thought she saw a touch of sadness in her sister's eyes and wondered what was behind it.

'Here we go.' Chad's deep voice over her shoulder made Maggie jump. 'Careful. We don't need to add emergency room stitches to the list of today's disasters.'

She stood back and let him set the heavy mirror in place. For the next ten minutes they worked in companionable silence as Chad anticipated what she needed and Maggie couldn't help wondering if he was the same in all areas of his life.

'Looks pretty damn good I'd say.'

She examined it from every angle and couldn't argue.

'Wow!'

Maggie glanced up at Fiona and almost wept with relief as a broad smile lit up her old friend's face.

'This is so unique. I've never seen this at a wedding before.' Satisfaction oozed through her voice. 'We'll start a whole new trend.'

Chad gave her a long slow wink behind Fiona's back and it was all Maggie could do not to giggle.

'When Emily told me you'd changed the cake I wasn't convinced it was a good idea. In fact I got a tiny bit cross, even though you are my best friend.'

A tiny bit cross wasn't quite how her sister described Fiona's meltdown but Maggie held her tongue.

'But she talked up the idea so convincingly I gave in. She told me how brilliant you were and swore that you'd soon be the most sought after wedding cake creator in the country.'

'She did?' Maggie couldn't hide her amazement.

'She admires you so much. Emily said anybody could cook, but what you did was beyond special.'

Was it stupid to believe for a single second that her sister might have meant what she said for once? *Yes, it is, remember all the times she's made a fool of you.*

'I love the whole thing,' Fiona declared and flung her arms around Emily. Suddenly she let go and gave Chad a puzzled stare.

Maggie didn't know what to say as her friend glanced between the two of them, plainly trying to work out why he was hovering near them.

'You sure are a beauty today.' He treated her to his most charming smile and picked up Fiona's hand, lifting it to his lips for a kiss. 'Peter's a lucky man.'

Fiona turned traffic light red. *Impossible to resist, isn't he?*

'I hope you're enjoying yourself?' Fiona asked. 'How are you getting on with everyone at your table? Peter's mother wanted to put you with their other relatives but he was sure you'd prefer this. Maggie tried to convince me not to do the 'singles table' thing but I don't see anything wrong with it,' she rattled on, 'I met Peter at a friend's wedding when we were seated together and we fell madly in love on the spot.' Maggie winced and sneaked a quick glance at Chad. Amusement lurked in his eyes and she held her breath, pretty sure he wouldn't divulge the secret about how he'd actually been spending his time.

'Everyone's been amazing,' he declared with another broad grin. 'I saw Maggie struggling with a heavy mirror and came over to give her a hand. I'd better return to my seat. Don't want to miss the speeches.' With a nod to them both he left.

Anyone would think he couldn't wait to be bored to death. Maggie decided Chad Robertson was an expert dissembler. She'd do well to remember that.

6

Finally he had no choice. The Reject Table it was, for better or worse. He'd have to leave tracking Maggie down again until later. A minute ago she hadn't been sure what he would say in front of Fiona and Chad wanted more than anything to convince her to trust him. *Why? What're you going to do about it? Nothing.* The problem was timing.

He'd read somewhere once that finding true love was all a question of timing. It had to be right on both sides for a long-term relationship to stand a chance of working. Up until now he'd always been the one dragging his heels as his failure to sustain anything long-term proved. He wasn't sure why he was that way but suspected being surrounded by long, good marriages on both sides of his family had made him afraid of screwing up the Robertson track record. Six months seemed to be the point when women started making plans for Christmas or vacations together and he automatically got scared and wanted out.

You'd happily sit around a Christmas tree with Maggie or fly her off for a week's fun on a sun-drenched exotic beach. Admit it.

Thinking of Maggie in a skimpy bikini, something sapphire-blue and clinging, wasn't smart and Chad contemplated a vacation to the Antarctic instead to cool himself down.

'Well, if it isn't our missing guest.'

He stopped, surprised to find himself standing next to his assigned table without any memory of getting there. Chad automatically smiled at the blonde pouting her blood-red lips in his direction and launched into an abject apology. He introduced himself to everyone else, mentally taking notes to repeat to Maggie later. *If she gives you the chance.*

Tonya — blonde divorcee looking for husband number three. Great Aunt Audrey — disapproving of the behaviour of modern young people and not afraid to say so. Peregrine Worthing — pale-faced organist wearing a well-worn corduroy jacket and tweed slacks. Two giggling girlfriends of the bride — one named Pippa and the other Pansy — for the life of him Chad couldn't tell them apart.

'Come and sit down and tell us your story.' Tonya patted the chair next to her, tossing her hair in what Chad was no doubt supposed to consider a sexy way. He gave her one of his patent smiles and settled himself down.

This woman didn't realise she was up against an expert. Any man who could successfully deflect Elizabeth 'Sunny' Donelson was no lightweight. The Nashville socialite had considered her outrageous bid of $50,000 at the bachelor auction entitled her to far more than his agreed to evening out on the town. Not even for the Vanderbilt Children's Hospital would he do some of the things she'd suggested but he'd managed to turn her down in such a way that they'd enjoyed the evening and were now firm friends.

'I'd much rather hear about you,' he murmured. Chad could be kind without encouraging her the wrong way, it wouldn't kill him. Tonya launched into a diatribe about her ex-husbands and he itched to tell her to stop. Nothing was less enticing to a man than hearing the rest of his sex trashed. 'Tell me what I should see while I'm here. I only came a couple of days ago and I've got until next Wednesday to explore Cornwall.' As soon as the words were out he regretted them. If she offered to show him around he'd better come up with an excuse and pronto. He hadn't been able to think of anything else on the spur of the moment to change the track of the conversation.

'It's the dullest place on the planet,'

she sniped, 'I'm moving back to London as soon as I can sell my house. You'd be better off spending your time in London rather than this dump.'

He exhaled a silent sigh of relief that he wasn't going to be offered a tour guide. Someone poked his arm and Chad turned towards the elderly lady on his left.

'Don't listen to her,' she commanded. 'The girl hasn't a whit of sense. She's proved that with the brainless idiots she married.' Tonya started to protest but was silenced with a withering glance. 'Do you have any interest in Celtic history or gardens or literature?' Her perceptive gaze swept over him. 'Or are you another empty-headed Yank with more money than sense?'

Chad was too amused by her blunt manner to be offended. Audrey would give his own sharp-tongued grand-mother a run for her money. 'I'm pretty sure I've a fair amount of both, ma'am,' he drawled. 'As well as my law degree I also have an art degree. Early twentieth century English design, in particular ceramics, is my specialty. I've inherited my mother's love of gardening, I practise music rights law and run a sub-four hour marathon.' *Touche.* A tinge of colour flushed her papery skin and Chad didn't regret a word. If he'd been humble and modest Audrey would've chewed him up and spat him out.

Everyone else around the table joined in the conversation and suggestions flew around until he had enough things to do in Cornwall to keep him busy from now until he turned ninety. As he was finding out more about the Eden Project from Pansy, or maybe it was Pippa, someone banged a gong and called for quiet.

Chad scanned the room for Maggie and smiled as he spotted her, cake knife in hand, by the famous wedding cake. He caught her eye and winked.

'Don't you dare mess Maggie around.' Audrey turned from pleasant to fierce in one second.

'I didn't realise you two were related?' *In other words, mind your own business.*

'Watch your tongue, young man. Maggie is my god-daughter and she and Fiona grew up almost like sisters, more so than that whippet of a girl prancing around with the food today.' *Emily's not your favourite person?* 'She hasn't had an easy life and doesn't need you flashing your far-too-white teeth at her in that wolfish smile.' *Wolfish smile?*

'I admire Maggie very much and 'messing around' isn't on my agenda,' he spoke firmly, holding the old woman's stare until she blinked first. 'If you don't mind I'd prefer to concentrate on the speeches now.' Chad turned away. Her piqued expression made it clear he'd irritated her but she could hardly condemn him for displaying good manners. One point to him.

★ ★ ★

Maggie hated being so aware of Chad. Ever since she came out of the kitchen to help with the cake-cutting she'd tried not to stare in his direction. Seeing his head bent close to Tonya and watching him laugh had annoyed her no end but then he'd got the whole table talking until they were obviously having more fun than everyone else in the room. He even charmed Great Aunt Audrey into smiling more than once. The Chad-named Reject Table was obviously a million miles from the usual pitiful place.

Fiona's father stood up to make his speech and after a minute or two Maggie was biting back tears. Childhood memories flooded back as Mr Jennings told stories about his only daughter, many of which featured Maggie too. She glanced at Chad and he met her eyes, his sympathetic smile helped her to suck in a calming breath as Mr Jennings finished and sat back down. The groom came next and emotion overwhelmed her again as

Peter spoke eloquently about his love for his new wife. Maggie didn't want to be a jealous cow, but couldn't help wondering if any man would ever declare her to be the centre of his world. She stared down at her feet, incongruously deciding she really needed a new pair of shoes. While Peter finished and Jack, the best man, started his speech, she continued to focus on the floor.

'Now Fiona and Peter will cut the cake. Word of warning, mate, be careful of women with sharp knives,' Jack teased and Maggie snapped to, realising she needed to stop moping.

With the cake cut she loaded up trays with the famous cake jars ready for Emily and her crew to pass around.

'Go and sit down. Take ten minutes,' Emily whispered in her ear and Maggie tried to protest but her sister shooed her away. 'Drool over your American while you have the chance.'

Suddenly shy, Maggie put her hands up to her hot shiny cheeks. Her hair must be even more of a mess now and if she took off her apron it'd reveal her tight, creased dress. Compared to the glossy, well-groomed girls at Chad's table she was a wreck.

'You're beautiful.' Chad's honeyed drawl in her ear startled her and only his hand on her elbow stopped her from tripping over her own feet as she turned around.

'And you're an inveterate liar.'

His tawny eyes darkened. 'Don't say that,' Chad teased. 'I was only speaking the truth as I see it.'

Maggie swallowed hard. 'Sorry.'

'You're safe. I won't hurt you because if I do Audrey will skin me alive.' His quirky smile made her laugh out loud.

'She's a tough old lady.'

Chad pushed a strand of her loose hair back out of the way. 'You might call her old. I value my life too much. She reminds me of my own grandmother.'

'The one who forced you to come to the wedding?'

His searing gaze bored into her and

Maggie couldn't make herself look away. 'I'll be forever grateful for the fact she's a determined woman.' He ran his thumb down over her cheek, lingering on her jaw and sending delightful shivers running through her blood. 'My favourite kind.'

'I've only got ten minutes, how about we sit down and taste the fruits of our hard work?'

Chad glanced over his shoulder and turned back to her with a shrug. 'I suppose we'd better go and join the others at the table although I'd rather have you to myself.'

Was he always this frank?

'Yeah, I pretty much tell it like it is, sweetheart.' His eyes sparkled, drawing her in as he'd done from the moment they met. 'Many of my clients hire me for that very reason, although occasionally I have to restrain myself.'

'I bet that's a challenge,' Maggie teased and an appealing flush highlighted his sharp cheekbones.

'No comment.'

'A very lawyerly answer.'

'Sure is.' He held out his hand. 'Come on, we're wasting cake eating time.'

'A sacrilege if ever I heard one.' Recklessly she placed her hand in his, not caring who saw.

Chad led her across the room and Maggie felt more than a few pairs of eyes following their progress.

'Here's our other reject come to join the fun,' he announced with a wide grin around at the disparate group who'd all stopped eating to stare at them.

7

'Sit by me,' Audrey ordered, gesturing at the seat next to her. 'You look worn out, Margaret. I want an explanation for why we're eating cake out of jam jars. Last week Fiona described every detail of the cake she'd ordered and *this* isn't it.' She prodded the mixture as if it contained arsenic.

Creative culinary experiments were plainly out of the old lady's realm. Chad caught Maggie's eye and she gave a resigned shrug. They both knew Audrey would demand the truth, the whole truth and nothing but the truth.

'Do something useful, young man, and fetch this poor girl a drink.' Audrey swivelled around to face him.

'Yes, ma'am.' Chad swiftly agreed and hurried off to collar one of the waitresses, persuading her to fetch him a bottle of champagne. He returned to the table brandishing the bottle and caught snippets of Maggie's muttered conversation with the older lady. By the sharp glances Audrey kept throwing his way Chad guessed his part in the kitchen proceedings wasn't a secret any more. He poured a fresh glass out for Maggie and topped up everyone else's.

'There you go.' Chad raised his glass. 'I think we should all drink a toast to our wonderful cake magician.'

Tonya's cool stare was distinctly less friendly now. He hadn't missed her watching when he and Maggie walked to the table together. Holding her hand might not have been wise but he didn't regret giving in to his impulse.

'Sit there.' Audrey gestured to the chair on her other side and Chad did as he was told. 'Is your sister behaving herself?'

'Emily's fine, thank you.' Maggie glanced at her watch. 'I must get back to the kitchen soon. There's lots to do.'

Audrey's shrewd dark eyes narrowed. 'Very convenient, my dear. I expect you to come and have tea with me one day next week so we can have a proper conversation.' She gave a sharp nod in Chad's direction. 'Bring him along. He'll enjoy seeing my house and we might teach him how to drink tea the proper way.'

The helpless glance he received said Maggie didn't have a clue how to reply.

'We'd be delighted.' Chad oozed Southern charm as if he'd been born on a Mississippi plantation and spent his days drinking mint juleps on the front porch. 'It sure is kind of you to invite me to your home. All I ask is that you let down the drawbridge and order the guards to hold back on the boiling oil.' Maggie stifled a giggle and he squeezed her hand under the table.

'You are a very cheeky man, Mr Robertson.' Her haughty manner was completely at odds with the smile tugging at the edges of her narrow lips. 'Monday at three. And don't be late. I abhor unpunctuality even more than being answered back to.'

'Monday it is. Should we synchronise our watches now?' Chad teased.

Maggie jumped up to standing. 'Some of us have work to do. I'll leave you two to trade insults to your heart's content.' She leaned down and kissed the old lady's cheek. 'I'll see you on Monday.' Straightening up she nodded at him. 'Behave yourself.'

'Yes, ma'am.' Judging by Maggie's mischievous smile she'd love to say more but didn't dare. 'Off you go. I'll catch up with you later.'

'I'm sure you will,' she muttered, hurrying away before Chad could say anymore. She'd noticed him stifle a smile when Audrey called her Margaret. No one else called her that these days although her parents had always insisted on doing so. She blinked back tears. How they'd love to be here today and see she and Emily working together. *It's not by choice. Admit it.*

When Emily first broached the idea Maggie's heart had sunk. She'd been making wedding cakes for several years in addition to her regular job with a local estate agent and on the verge of saving enough to start her own business. Emily had flitted her way through more jobs than anyone could remember without settling to anything and when she turned on the guilt screw Maggie had succumbed.

Please, Maggie. You know I'm not smart like you with money. I can cook but you're good at bossing people around and organising things. Mum and Dad would be so pleased. They always wanted us to be closer.

Their father had never appeared to see past Emily's helpless princess act, but a couple of times Maggie suspected that her mother did. From the time she was old enough to understand it'd been made clear to Maggie that she was responsible for Emily, not the other way around. Dad had explained it very gently.

Some people are born tough and others aren't, Margaret. She can't help being sensitive and emotional. You'll have to help her navigate the world because other people won't always understand.

Maggie hadn't really understood either, but even at eight-years-old knew not to say so out loud. Life wasn't ever easy. She sighed to herself and slipped back into the kitchen — walking straight into another nightmare.

★ ★ ★

'You want to steer clear of Maggie,' Tonya whispered in Chad's ear. 'The family's unstable. Her sister's a bit of a loony.'

Chad sipped his champagne and set the glass back down on the table. Tonya Egerton plainly still fancied her chances with him and wasn't about to prise her claws out in a hurry.

'You sure have a wild imagination.' He gave no hint of the anger bubbling under his surface smile. 'What do you plan to do in London when you move back there?' Chad tried to change the subject.

Tonya smirked. 'Oh, dear, you do have it bad.'

He hated being seen through by this unpleasant woman and glanced in Audrey's direction only to catch her giving him an equally knowing look.

'Maggie will probably be very *grateful* later.' Tonya wouldn't let it go and Chad's hands tensed around his champagne glass.

'I suggest you keep your uncharitable thoughts to yourself, young lady.' Audrey's imperious tones rang out and everyone around them stared. 'Your parents would be ashamed to hear you talking that way.'

An angry flush coloured Tonya's neck and crept up to flood her face. Chad almost wished the old lady had kept her mouth shut. Experience told him this woman wasn't someone you wanted as an enemy. He had a suspicion she could cause trouble for Maggie if she chose to.

'Let's not spoil a good wedding,' Chad chirped, inwardly wincing at his fake good humour. 'Maybe we haven't had enough champagne yet.' He picked up the bottle and refilled Tonya's glass and his own.

Audrey held a hand over the top of her glass and fixed the other woman with a stony glare. 'Some people have had too much already, and that's part of the problem.'

Chad set the bottle back down and wondered how much longer the reception would last. He was only grateful there was no evening party to get through because avoiding Tonya's clutches on the dance floor might've been beyond even his expertise. He didn't go much on his chances of seeing Maggie again later because he could hardly hang around while she cleared up after Emily's earlier scathing remarks. He suddenly realised they were the only three left on the Reject Table. The two younger girls had gravitated towards a couple of the ushers and were attempting to work their magic on the luckless men. The organist was nowhere to be seen and Chad guessed he'd slipped away to feed his cat or practise the hymns for tomorrow's service.

Chandler, I'm disappointed in you. The poor man did nothing to deserve your unkindness.

His mother's quiet reprimand filled his head and Chad wordlessly murmured an apology, to his parent and the absent organist. One thing his parents were always strict with him and Josh about was the need to treat everyone the same. It didn't matter if they were a garbage collector or the President of the United States.

Out of the blue a piercing scream rang out from the kitchen and Chad leapt to his feet, shoved the chair back out of the way and wended his way through the staggered rows of tables, pushing one man out of the way Chad threw open the kitchen door and froze.

Maggie, wide-eyed and frighteningly pale, was bent down over her sister's lifeless figure sprawled on the floor.

'Has someone called for an ambulance?' He shouted and one of the waitresses shook her head. 'Why not?'

'Because I told her not to.' Maggie's voice was barely audible but a note of steel ran through every word. 'I need to get Emily home.'

The attorney in him wanted to ask more questions, and press her until he got the truth but he didn't dare. 'Do you need any help?'

She glanced up and her deep blue eyes shone with tears. 'No, thank you. I can manage.' *I've had to plenty of other times*. Her unspoken words rang out so clearly he flinched.

'How about with clearing away after the reception finishes?' *Anything. Tell me and I'll do it.*

'Susan will see to everything.' Maggie nodded towards an older red-haired waitress hovering nearby.

What else could he do? Chad nodded. 'I'll call later and check y'all are okay.'

'Please don't bother. I'll be busy.'

He fished out a silver business card case from his pocket and opened it to pass one over to her. 'Use this number if you need anything. I mean it.' Chad met her challenging stare before he turned and walked away. Back to the Reject Table.

8

'What am I going to do?' Emily wailed. 'He's got cross at me a few times recently and we did have a bit of an argument yesterday but I never thought he'd actually *leave* me.' Maggie wrapped her arms around her sister and rocked her until the heaving sobs quietened down. 'He dumped me by text. By *text*. What sort of man does that?'

One who knows how emotional you are and can't cope. He knew this was how you'd react and was too much of a coward to face it himself. Instead he'd left Maggie to pick up the pieces.

'A weak one, Ems. And not good enough for you.' Maggie stroked Emily's silky golden hair. No matter how annoying her sister could be she didn't deserve to be treated this way — no one did. 'Let's get you home.'

Emily gazed wide-eyed around the room at the rest of the staff who were watching them with unconcealed interest.

'Can you stand up?' Maggie asked, getting a brief nod in return. She let go of her sister and scrambled to her feet, holding out her hand to help Emily. 'Okay?' She caught Susan's eye. 'Are you sure you can cope?'

'It's not a problem. The bride and groom are due to leave in ten minutes. The reception will break up then.' Susan reassured her. 'Don't worry. You see to Emily and I'll ring you tomorrow.'

'Thanks.' She turned back to see her sister, pale as a ghost and shaking. Even Emily couldn't fake this level of distress and for once she genuinely felt sorry for her. 'I'll get my handbag and we'll be off.' Maggie led her sister towards the back door of the kitchen. They'd have to walk around to the front of the hotel where her car was parked but it was better than going out through the reception crowd and attracting too much attention. *You can't stand to see Chad again, can you?* He'd been nothing but kind and she'd thrown his sympathy right back in his face. 'Come on, Ems,' she encouraged and her sister trailed along behind her. They made it to the car and briefly Maggie considered and quickly rejected the idea of going back in to say goodbye to Fiona and Peter. She fastened Emily's seatbelt and hurried around to get in the driver's seat. For a second she clung onto the wheel and took a couple of slow, deep breaths.

'Are you alright?'

Somehow she managed to nod at hearing her sister's unexpected concern and started up the car. Maggie headed off down the long gravel driveway and drove the ten miles to their house without either of them saying another word.

* * *

'Spill the beans.' Tonya's eyes gleamed at Chad. 'Let me guess. Loopy Emily broke a fingernail?'

Maggie's sister was obviously renowned for being a drama queen, but Chad was pretty sure there was more to it this time.

'That's quite enough.' Audrey interrupted, 'There's a Jewish proverb that goes 'What you don't see with your eyes, don't witness with your mouth'.' Her sharp gaze focused on Chad, clearly telling him not to indulge Tonya's curiosity.

'I have no idea, but everything seems to be fine now,' he replied, although it wasn't anywhere near the truth. Chad wasn't stupid, despite the older woman's concern and had no intention of saying anything that could be repeated or misconstrued. The loud boom of the gong silenced the room and saved him from being interrogated any more. Fiona's father encouraged everyone to head outside to see off the newly married couple.

Chad jumped to his feet. 'Ladies, may I escort you?' He flashed one of his brightest smiles. Tonya instantly sprung to her feet and wriggled her hand through his arm so he couldn't shake her off without being rude. Chad offered his other arm to Audrey and her face creased in a half smile. Graciously she allowed him to tuck her hand into his elbow and he steered the three of them out through the crowd.

'You're a very good liar, Mr Robertson,' Audrey whispered. 'I don't wish to know what happened, but I am worried about those girls.'

'I honestly don't know the full story, but Maggie seemed to be handling it okay,' he murmured, turning his head so Tonya couldn't catch their conversation.

'She's always had to.' Audrey shook her head. 'It's wicked that their parents made Maggie responsible for her sister when there's nothing wrong with Emily a good spanking as a child wouldn't have cured.'

This wasn't the time or place to discuss Maggie's upbringing despite his overwhelming urge to know more. He turned back to Tonya. 'Any idea where the happy couple are honeymooning?'

'I did hear they were going to Hawaii, but have no idea if that's right.' She leaned forward to give Audrey a snide nod. 'I probably shouldn't have told you because it's only the *gossip* going around.'

'Don't try to be clever, my dear, it doesn't suit you.' Audrey's sharp tone made Chad wince. Why did he get stuck trying to negotiate peace between two of the most difficult women in the room while the one he really wanted to be with had soundly rejected him?

They joined the crowd gathered around the front door of the hotel and Chad's fervent hope was that Fiona and Peter would hurry up and leave. As soon as the confetti throwing was over he intended to politely get rid of his two companions. He'd escape to the local pub where he was staying, dump the fancy suit and drown his sorrows at the bar. Chad had managed to weasel out of Peter's mother's invitation to join them for a family meal later by pleading jet-lag. Lying wasn't honourable, especially to his family, but he'd had more than enough for one day.

*   *   *

Maggie watched Emily's peaceful breathing. As soon as they'd had a cup of tea her sister had fallen asleep on the sofa. At least it meant she didn't have to keep listening to heartbroken, unanswerable questions about Jonathan's reasons for breaking off their engagement. Maggie's educated guess was that he'd got tired of babying Emily but what did she know? Her own experience with men could fit on the head of the proverbial pin. In between keeping an eye on Emily, earning a living and trying to get a business started the amount of time she'd had for a social life was close to nil. To say that the majority of the dates she had been on were less than stellar successes was putting it mildly.

Emily wouldn't wake for a while so Maggie decided to take a chance. She hurried up to her bedroom, desperate to change out of the tight dress she'd been crammed into all day. As she pulled the zip down her body sagged with joy and settled back into its natural curves. Maggie tossed the offending object on her chair ready to take to the dry cleaners on Monday. Her stalwart dress was at least ten years old and had been to so many weddings Maggie was surprised it didn't receive its own invitation. She tugged on an old elastic-waist floral skirt and a plain white blouse and shoved her aching feet into her ancient pink slippers. Next she shook out the contents of the small black bag she'd carried to the wedding and started to to transfer everything back into the cavernous linen satchel she used most of the time.

From the middle of the pile Maggie picked up Chad's business card. She toyed with it and wondered what he'd say if she rang him. *You know what he'd say. He'd be concerned. Ask if you're alright and whether he could do anything to help. Want to see you again.* She let herself remember Chad's tempting smile, the aroma of his delicious spicy cologne and the way he'd rolled up his sleeves and gone to work as if he always went to weddings and ended up helping to make the cake.

He was out of her league, if she even had a league, and it'd been a ridiculous notion from the beginning. Sometimes even her sensible, responsible self behaved foolishly at weddings — maybe it was something about all that love and hopeful optimism flying around.

'Maggie, where are you?' Emily's panicked voice drifted up the stairs. She plunged back to earth. This was her life, not whatever glamorous existence Mr Chad Robertson led back in Nashville, Tennessee.

'Coming, Ems. I was just changing.' Apart from her clothes nothing else was going to alter anytime soon.

9

'What are you doing here?' Maggie glared out at Chad from the safety of her half-open front door. It wasn't exactly the warm welcome he'd hoped for.

'I came to see how you're doing. I'll go away again if you want.'

'You've been drinking.' She frowned and peered out around him. 'How did you get here?'

'I flew,' he said dryly. 'Believe it or not I discovered Cornwall has taxis, the same as most of the civilised world.' The tight line of her mouth deepened and he guessed she was fighting against giving in to a smile.

'In that case I suggest you ring them right now to take you back to wherever you came from and leave me alone.'

Chad leaned against the door and caught a hint of Maggie's delicious scent, the intoxicating mixture of vanilla and warm, soft woman driving him crazy. 'Is that *really* what you want?'

'Do you honestly think I need a half-drunk man on my doorstep on top of all my other problems?' Maggie snapped.

'Honey, don't be too hard on me. I only had a couple shots of Jack Daniels for courage.'

'Courage?'

'To disobey you,' he muttered. 'I know you told me to go away, but I hated seeing you upset and I couldn't damn well go to bed not knowing if you were okay.' That was the surface reason, and a genuine one, but underneath a myriad of others fought for his attention. 'You gonna let me in?'

'Maggie, is that . . . oh, it's you.' Emily's forlorn face crumpled as she appeared at the door and spotted him. 'I hoped Jonathan had come back.'

'Do you get it now that I don't have time for you as well as all this?' Maggie's brutal tone cut him to the bone.

'I'm going to bed.' Emily whispered. 'Maybe when I wake up in the morning this will all be a nightmare.' She slouched off back into the house. Chad took a chance and rested his hand on Maggie's arm, saying nothing. A single large tear trickled down her cheek and he tenderly brushed it away. 'Would it help to talk?'

She shook her head, nodded several times and then shook it again. 'I . . . don't know.'

'How about I come in, make you a cup of tea and then you can decide?' he suggested, mentally crossing his fingers.

'Do you even *know* how to make tea?' Her voice wobbled, but the faintest trace of a smile pulled at her generous mouth.

'I sure do,' Chad asserted with more confidence than he actually felt. The same legal mentor who'd recommended always replying to one question with another also told him never to sound as though he didn't know what he was talking about in court. 'Boiling water. Tea. China cup. Milk and sugar if required. Cake.'

Maggie's deep blue eyes sparkled. 'I think we've had more than enough cake for one day, don't you?'

'Is there such a thing as too much cake?'

★ ★ ★

'You're far too clever.' Maggie wagged her finger at him. 'Nobody should be able to make me smile right now.' *But the problem is looking at you makes me happy and I can't seem to help it.* A lock of black hair fell over Chad's forehead and she yearned to stroke it back into place, except that it looked far too tempting where it was.

A satisfied grin crept over his face as it dawned on him she wasn't going to send him away — not yet. She'd turned down everyone's offers of help but he'd ignored her and turned up anyway. Chad wasn't stupid so he had to be as stubborn as she was. When she was fifteen Maggie didn't eat for three days because her father wouldn't let her go to a Save the Whales demonstration in London. Her exasperated mother said she might as well resign herself to being an old maid because no man would put up with such a pig-headed girl.

'I suppose you'd better come in.' Maggie worked on sounding as ungracious as possible. She didn't need him to think she was falling at his feet. She strode away down the hall into the kitchen and by the sound of heavy footsteps on the bare wood floor behind her assumed Chad was following. Maggie filled the kettle at the sink before switching it on.

'Are you rejecting my tea-making offer?' Chad teased.

'You may think you sounded sure of yourself but I saw right through you. I'd bet on my most precious possession that you've never made a decent cup of tea in your life.' His dark gaze swept down over her and Maggie shivered in an unexpected, good sort of way.

He folded his arms and she suddenly became aware he'd changed out of the fancy suit. Only a thin red T-shirt covered his broad chest and Chad's jeans were more holes than denim, emphasising his long, muscular legs.

'I'll take your bet,' he drawled, his voice running all over her skin like a puddle of golden syrup melting over hot buttered toast.

'You don't even know what I'm talking about,' Maggie protested.

'I don't need to, sugar, if it's important to you I might lose on purpose.' He took a step closer and she struggled to keep breathing, far too aware of his clean, masculine scent surrounding her. Chad rested a finger on her jaw and lifted her chin to meet his smouldering eyes. 'You willin' to take the chance?'

She was pretty sure they weren't talking about tea any longer. A sudden image of Emily's distraught face flashed in front of Maggie's eyes and she reluctantly pushed Chad away. 'I don't need this,' she whispered.

'I didn't mean to be heartless. I only wanted to make you smile again.'

Overreacting was usually Emily's prerogative and a wave of guilt swept through Maggie. 'Sorry. I'm being a cow.'

'Nope, you aren't.' He shook his head. 'It's been a long, tough day all around.' Chad pulled out a chair and gently pushed her to sit down. 'I'll make your tea. No bets. No flirting. Simply tea.'

Maggie couldn't decide if she was sorry or not.

He turned away and began to make a pot of tea, with the same quiet concentration she'd observed earlier during the cake disaster episode. At first she'd been surprised to hear he was a lawyer but now with his smooth talking charm, quick brain and attention to detail it made complete sense. For the first time in hours Maggie let herself relax.

'Hey, tired girl, do you want tea or a nap?'

Her eyes flew open and it took a second for her to register Chad's concerned face inches away from hers. 'What are you talking about?' Maggie rubbed at her eyes.

'If I hadn't put my hand out to keep you on the chair you'd be flat on the floor by now.' He said with a wry smile. 'You're exhausted.'

'Tea please.' Maggie murmured, glancing away so she didn't have to meet his intense eyes, the flecks of brown and gold shimmering in the light.

'Yes, ma'am.' The touch of sarcastic humour made her smile despite everything. 'Strong, weak, milk, sugar, lemon — specific details please and I'll fix it for you.'

'Strong. A little milk. No sugar.'

'Your wish is my command.' Chad teased and proceeded to follow her instructions. 'There you go.' He set a cup down in front of Maggie and poured another one for himself before joining her. They both started to drink and she waited for him to start bugging her with questions.

'It's complicated,' Maggie blurted out and caught him half-smile. The damn man was too clever. He'd purposely kept quiet and the silence forced her to speak up.

'People usually are.' His free hand rested on the table and without thinking she covered it with her own. She rubbed idly over the dusting of dark hair, buoyed by the strength and warmth under her stroking fingers. 'Don't tell me any more than you're comfortable with. I'm happy to listen as much as you want but I don't want you to regret it in the morning.'

His ambiguous words made her cheeks burn with embarrassment.

'You've got a wicked mind.' He chuckled and shook his head in fake disappointment, but in a flash his smile faded. 'Sorry. I promised no flirting.'

Would it be awful to tell him she really didn't mind?

'Of course, if you . . . '

She leaned over and placed her finger on his mouth, silencing him. 'Leave it.' Maggie sat back and took another large swallow of her tea. A shy smile warmed his eyes making her glad he'd stayed. Having no one to talk through things with was tough and for some absurd reason she trusted Chad.

'Do you wanna start with what Emily was upset about earlier?'

Maggie plunged in before she could change her mind. 'Her fiancé, Jonathan, sent her a text breaking off their engagement.'

'What a shit.' She gasped at his harsh comment. 'Sorry, excuse my language.'

'That didn't shock me, it's the fact you reduced it to the basic truth. Nothing else really matters because there's no excuse for his behaviour, is there?'

Chad shook his head. 'Nope.'

She started to fill in a few details, telling him how Emily and Jonathan met a couple of years ago and how kind and patient he'd been with her sister's uncertain temperament. At least until recently when his tolerance appeared to be fraying around the edges. Chad raised his eyebrows, but didn't say a word. Maggie explained that they'd been planning a spring wedding and Emily had bought her wedding dress already. 'She kept on at him last week to set a date but he didn't answer her outright. I wonder if he felt cornered?'

'I guess it could be.' Chad shrugged and didn't quite meet her eyes. 'You don't suppose there's . . . well, you know . . . '

'Another woman?'

He nodded.

'I suppose it's possible, but I suspect it's more a question of him getting tired of trying to handle Emily's ups and downs.' *God knows, I'd understand that. Sometimes I can't either.*

Chad's eyes darkened and she watched him working out how to phrase his next question.

10

'Spit it out. You don't have to creep around me. I don't do tears and hysterics. There isn't room for more than one of those in a family.'

Chad decided to take Maggie at her word. Sometimes clients asked him to be honest and meant it, others spoke the words but it was the last thing they really wanted. But everything about Maggie had been straightforward from the moment they met. 'Has Emily always been very emotional?' A heavy silence swirled around them. Maggie nodded, her shoulders drooping with tired sadness.

'My first memory is of Emily throwing a tantrum in a shoe shop. She threw shoes around, kicked the assistant and screamed the place down because my mother wouldn't let her have the inappropriate pair she wanted.

Of course Mum gave in and bought them.'

'So she learned how to manipulate people and get her own way and hasn't ever grown out of it.'

Maggie shrugged. 'I was told she was sensitive and artistic so my job was to be the responsible one and look out for her.' Resentment threaded through her words. 'I do love her, but I . . . '

Chad picked up her hands, rubbing them with his own to warm up her chilled skin. They were the hands of a woman used to work, strong and capable and he admired that. He might be an attorney but could still plumb a toilet and build a wall from the ground up. His father insisted they knew how to take care of themselves and the fact they could afford to pay other people to do things was irrelevant.

'Of course you do, but there's no shame in admitting she sometimes frustrates you and you wish things could be different.' For a second he almost shared his story about his own strained relationship with his brother but she didn't need his burdens added to her own. 'It's put a damper on your choices, hasn't it?' *Like with me today.*

'Sometimes.'

The tight line of her mouth told Chad he might've gone too far, too soon. 'Would it help if you got in touch with Jonathan?'

Maggie screwed up her face. 'I can't see how.'

'Maybe you could persuade him to speak to Emily face to face and explain his reasons for breaking off the engagement.'

'You're behaving as if it was me or you this was happening to,' she scoffed. 'Emily would tear his eyes out.'

For the first time Chad wondered if the other man wasn't so dumb after all, even though he'd taken the coward's way out.

'You think he was right, don't you?' she accused, and he couldn't lie outright.

'Not exactly, but . . . '

'There are no buts.' She jerked her hands away.

Now he'd upset her, which was the last thing he wanted.

'It's late and I'm very tired,' Maggie declared. 'You'd better leave.'

Chad debated arguing his case, but there was no point. They were both worn out and he had no right to challenge a woman he barely knew over the right way to run her life. His own wasn't exactly something to shout about. The stubborn side of him refused to totally quit. He had four more days left in Cornwall and wasn't ready to give up on Maggie Taylor yet. 'Fair enough. I'll be off.' She looked about to say something but slammed her lips shut again. Chad decided to give it one last try. 'If Emily's all right in the morning would you have lunch with me tomorrow? I'm staying at the Black Prince and everyone tells me their Sunday lunches are excellent.' Chad held his breath.

'I'll probably have to stay here to

keep her company,' she explained, but without any sign of her previous anger.

'But if you don't?' he persisted.

'If I don't I'll have lunch with you. All right?'

Chad grinned and held out his hand. 'Deal.' She took hold of it and he wrapped his fingers tightly around hers, giving a hard squeeze before letting go again. 'I'll call around mid-morning.'

'How are you going to get back to town? Do you want me to ring for a taxi?'

'The walk will do me good,' Chad declared and quickly got up and headed out to the front door. If he didn't work off some of his pent up energy he'd never sleep tonight. 'Good night.'

*　*　*

Maggie followed Chad with her eyes and it took all her self-control not to call out after him. She'd started off by telling him to go away and then almost agreed to have lunch with the man — it didn't make sense. Ever since she met him this morning he'd turned her life upside down. Maggie didn't do leaning on other people or opening up, both of which she'd done with a recklessness way beyond her understanding. He was leaving in a few days and a brief fling definitely wasn't on her agenda. She'd never been one for blink-and-you-miss-it relationships and still regretted the one night she'd succumbed as a teenager because she'd hated being considered odd and a prude. Maggie had promised herself the next time would be with a man she truly loved.

'Is Romeo gone?' Emily's voice drifted downstairs.

Maggie fought against sighing out loud at the sight of ashen-faced Emily wearing a voluminous white nightdress, and with her flowing blonde hair rippling around her shoulders. Presumably tonight her sister was channelling her inner Cathy pining over Heathcliff. At least it was calmer than the Lady Macbeth route.

'Chad has left, if that's what you mean.'

'I suppose you told him all about your useless sister?' Emily persisted, coming down to join her in the hall. 'I wouldn't blame you.'

Wouldn't you? You normally do. 'I didn't say much.' She chose her words with care because the last thing she needed was to set Emily off again.

'I don't suppose Jonathan called?'

Maggie shook her head.

'I didn't think so.'

'Do you want a cup of tea?'

Emily gave a hollow laugh. 'Tea? No, Maggie, tea isn't going to cure what's wrong this time.' She slapped a hand in front of her mouth and hurried away down the hall to run into the guest toilet. The unmistakeable sound of retching coming from behind the half-closed door made Maggie wince. *No lunch date tomorrow.*

Maggie returned to the kitchen and made a fresh pot of tea.

'You can pour me one too and I'll see

if I can keep it down,' Emily muttered, coming to join her.

'He's not worth making yourself ill over, he really isn't. I know you had your plans all made, but . . . '

'You don't get it do you?' She flung herself into the nearest chair. 'I'm pregnant, you idiot.' Emily burst into loud, wracking sobs.

Maggie crossed the room and bent down to wrap her arms around her sister's thin shoulders. How was she going to cope with this on top of everything else? Today's brief dream of Chad and the possibilities he dangled in front of her shattered into a million tiny pieces. 'It'll be okay. We'll manage.' She struggled to reassure herself as much as Emily. 'Does Jonathan know?'

'No.' Emily raised her head to look at Maggie, her eyes dark with pain.

'Why not?'

'Because I haven't told him,' she rushed on, 'I was going to after today's wedding but now there's no point.'

Of course there's a point. He's the

father. He's as responsible as you are and you've got to talk about this together.

'If he doesn't love me for myself then I don't want him to stay with me out of pity or duty,' Emily murmured, her words quiet but firm. 'You won't tell him, will you?'

'Not if you don't want me to, but I wish you'd reconsider. This is his baby as well as yours and he has a right to know.'

Her sister's features hardened into a stubborn mask. 'I'm not talking about it any more today.'

Maggie knew from bitter experience that when Emily dug her heels in nothing would budge her. She picked up the teapot and poured out another cup, adding milk and plenty of sugar before setting it quietly down in front of her sister. 'Try that.'

'Thanks.'

It was the closest she'd get to an apology. A wave of tiredness swept over her and all she wanted was to crawl into bed and sleep for a solid eight hours.

'I know I can be a bitch,' Emily murmured and fixed her wide, blue-eyed gaze on Maggie.

How was she supposed to respond? She was too tired to lie, but the truth might set off another meltdown and she couldn't cope with any more today.

'Don't say anything. Not now. I'm off back to bed,' Emily declared and pushed her chair back to stand up.

Maggie nodded and let her sister go. She didn't move straight away but simply sat there, listening to the rhythmic ticking of the kitchen clock and wondering how much harder her life could get.

11

Chad finished his second cup of coffee and picked up the phone. It was ten o'clock and he couldn't wait any longer to call Maggie. 'Good morning, beautiful.'

'I'm grateful we're not on Skype. I'm not even dressed yet.'

The mental picture of Maggie — warm, rumpled and wearing whatever skimpy attire she slept in didn't do his overwrought body any good. 'I'm trying to be a gentleman so I won't comment on *that*.'

'Did you get back okay last night?'

Her swift change of subject made him smile and Chad quickly assured her the walk hadn't killed him. 'Did you get a good night's sleep?' An odd silence filled the line.

'Sort of,' Maggie sighed. 'Things got more complicated after you left.'

He kept quiet and waited for her to explain.

'Is your offer still open?'

Which one? Chad mentally smacked himself. 'Lunch? Of course it is. Are you free?'

'Emily says she'll be fine so I'm taking her at her word.'

Bet that doesn't happen often. 'Great. I booked a table for one o'clock if that suits you?'

'Sure of yourself, weren't you?'

'Hey, a guy's got to eat. If you'd deserted me I'd be having a miserable, solitary lunch.' He relaxed again when Maggie laughed. 'I'll pick you up about twelve forty-five.'

'There's no need, I can . . . '

'Stop. Please. I was raised a good Southern boy and if I don't collect a lady properly for a date and return her safely afterwards my mother and daddy will haunt me forever.'

'Oh, did you lose your parents too? You never said.'

Chad groaned. 'I was teasing. My

parents are fine.' This was getting worse by the minute, now he'd made it sound as if them being dead would be a joke. 'That didn't come out right.'

'Look, I'll be ready. See you later.' Maggie stopped his rambling in her usual decisive manner.

Next thing he was holding a dead phone and smiling to himself.

⋆　⋆　⋆

Maggie dragged out an armful of clothes and flung them all over the bed. She hadn't been on a date for so long she didn't have a clue what to wear. Maybe she'd ring back and cancel. She could claim she'd been struck down with a sudden illness.

'It's only lunch.' Emily breezed in and dropped down to sit on the bed. 'Don't over think everything.'

Someone has to and you never do. 'How're you feeling?'

'Sick. Pregnant.' Emily nibbled on a cracker, dropping crumbs all over

Maggie's clothes and idly brushing them away. 'And don't fret about whether you can leave me alone.'

'But . . . '

'But nothing.' Emily picked up a multi-coloured skirt from the pile. 'God, this is ugly. Please tell me you're not wearing this hideous thing?' She selected another dress, an old summer floral Maggie loved and screwed up her nose. 'This does nothing for you. For God's sake give it to the charity shop.'

'For heaven's sake pick something.' Maggie gave up, throwing her hands in the air.

'Try these.' A black wraparound skirt and short-sleeved bright pink jumper, both bought recklessly in a sale but never worn, were tossed at her.

Maggie peeled off her bathrobe and picked up the skirt to step into it.

'Stop right there.' Emily's horrified shriek nearly made her wobble over. 'Please tell me you weren't going out in that awful ragged underwear?'

She gave an embarrassed glance

down over her worn out grey bra and stretchy granny knickers. 'What difference does it make? We're simply having Sunday lunch together and I'm not planning to be dished up as the pudding.'

'I would assume not, but you can't feel good wearing those disgusting things,' Emily persisted. 'Decent underwear gives you confidence from the inside out. Do you have anything that fits and isn't ten years old?'

Maggie opened the top drawer of her dresser and rifled around. 'How about these?' She held up a black lace bra and panty set she'd bought once in the hope of finding someone worth wearing them for.

'Not bad. They'll do. Get dressed.'

She did as she was told because it was easier than arguing.

'What about shoes?'

Maggie picked up the sensible ones she'd worn to yesterday's wedding and showed them to her sister, waiting to be vilified again.

Emily sighed and shook her head. 'You can fit into a size six can't you?'

'Maybe.'

'I'll lend you my Manolo Blahniks if you take care of them.' She hurried out of the room before Maggie could protest and soon returned, placing a pair of strappy black high-heeled shoes on the floor. 'There you go. I suppose my feet will be too puffy to wear them soon anyway,' she groused.

They were a little tight when she put them on but she didn't dare to complain.

Emily peered at her face. 'Are you wearing *any* make-up?'

'Enough.'

'At least let me find you a lipstick that matches.'

'Okay.' She waited patiently while her sister disappeared again and returned brandishing two tubes of lipstick. 'Sit.' Emily applied a rich dark pink layer to Maggie's lips and added a coat of shiny gloss. 'Stand up and look at yourself in the mirror.'

Maggie did as she was told, surprised by her reflection. 'Oh.' It was still her only more so.

'Much better, isn't it.' Emily smirked. 'You should make an effort more often. Now go and wait for your handsome suitor to arrive.'

'Thanks.' She hugged her sister, unable to express her gratitude sufficiently but hoping Emily might guess. The sisters-helping-each-other thing was an unknown experience for them and Maggie didn't want to break the fragile, new bond.

★   ★   ★

Chad's jaw dropped and he struggled not to ogle Maggie like a dirty old man. The softly draping skirt and pink top highlighted her feminine curves and her high heels drew his attention to a pair of shapely legs that'd been hidden under yesterday's ugly dress and apron. If her sister wasn't standing there like a Victorian chaperone he'd have already kissed the glossy pink layer off of Maggie's lush mouth.

'Do I have something stuck between my teeth?' Maggie asked and he managed to shake his head. 'Then why are you staring?'

Because you're the most beautiful woman on the planet and you don't have a clue how lovely you are. He caught Emily's eye and was surprised to receive a satisfied nod of approval. 'You look different without the apron.' Lame, but the best he could come up with so as not to humiliate himself in front of a woman he'd barely known for twenty-four hours.

'I would hope so.' Maggie's pithy remark made him smile. 'Are we going?'

'Of course.' Chad replied and then felt obliged to ask Emily to join them.

'Thanks, it's kind of you to offer but no. I'll be fine with my ginger ale and crackers.'

Weird, but he didn't comment, grateful to be turned down.

'Maggie will explain I'm sure, now off you go.' She shooed them away and disappeared towards the kitchen.

Chad led the way out to his car and helped Maggie in. Apart from thanking him she didn't say a word and all his attempts at conversation during the ten minute drive to the pub failed.

'This is the oldest pub in the area. I believe it dates back to about 1780,' Maggie said as they got out and walked inside.

He wasn't sure how to reply but thankfully the barman spotted him and asked them to go through to the dining room. Somehow they stumbled through choosing between roast beef, pork or lamb and decided on their drinks without really talking to each other.

Chad tried to think what topic of conversation to try next. His obvious admiration earlier must've freaked her out. 'Are we still on for tomorrow?' She threw him a puzzled look. 'Tea with the dragon lady.' When Maggie cracked a smile he almost cheered.

'It's practically a royal invitation and if we don't turn up on time and decently dressed it'll be the tower for us.'

'Your head is far too pretty to be stuck on a pike,' he joked, relieved when she joined in with his laughter.

Their appetisers arrived and when the waitress left Maggie stared down at her breaded mushrooms.

'Have I upset you somehow?' Chad needed to get this out in the open, whatever *this* was.

12

Maggie didn't know where to start without blubbering. Chad wanted pleasant, undemanding company for a few days not all the angst filling her life dumped on him. But the way he'd looked at her earlier had thrown her sideways. No man had ever done that before.

'No, you haven't done anything wrong.' *Except be a lovely man who's out of my reach.*

Chad gave her a shrewd, sweeping glance. 'Yesterday we got on well and I was looking forward to getting to know you better. I thought you felt the same, but maybe I was mistaken?'

She shook her head and swallowed hard.

'We both know I'm leaving on Wednesday, but that doesn't have to stop us . . . does it?' He picked up her hand, idly stroking her trembling fingers. 'Maggie.' His soft drawl lured her in again. 'Don't assume anything about me.'

'One beef and one lamb.'

Maggie jerked her hand away and struggled to pay attention to the waitress, holding out two plates and waiting for them to speak. 'The lamb is mine.'

For the next few minutes they had to tolerate being fussed over while sauces were fetched and glasses refilled until they were finally left alone again.

Chad tucked into his roast beef. 'This is delicious. British food is obviously much maligned.' A mischievous grin crept across his face. 'Well, except in the case of Scotch eggs.'

'Emily told me you weren't a fan.' Maggie smirked.

'That's an understatement, honey.' He put on a fake shudder and she found herself laughing again. 'That's much better.'

'What is?'

Chad rested his hand on her cheek. 'I love your laughter. It's so unrestrained and full of life.'

'You mean loud and common.'

His broad smile warmed her all the way down to her toes. 'Oh, Maggie Taylor, there's *nothing* common about you. You're unique.'

'I meant common as in uneducated and badly brought up,' she protested. 'You are such a lawyer, tying me up in knots.'

Chad's tawny eyes glowed and she couldn't make herself look away from him. 'I want you to be honest with me, whether it's by laughing at something you find funny or telling me why you're upset.'

She laid down her knife and fork. What did she have to lose? *Her dignity.* They wouldn't see each other again after Wednesday so what difference did it make?

'Emily's pregnant.' Maggie blurted it out and watched his eyes widen. 'She hasn't told Jonathan because she doesn't want him to come back to her out of pity. I don't know how I'm going to cope. Emily's acting differently towards me, nicer I suppose I'd say, and I'm not sure about that either.' She sucked in a deep breath. 'My life has enough complications without the fact I really like you.' Her voice trailed away and she wished she could crawl under the table and hide.

★ ★ ★

'I've always been one for complicated, and I *really* like you too so it's all good.' Chad lowered his voice. He couldn't resist reaching across and pressing a soft kiss on her flushed cheek, the hint of vanilla and warmth rising from her skin making him ache for so much more. 'How about we finish lunch and take our coffee out in the garden?' He gestured subtly towards the older couple at the next table flagrantly listening to their conversation.

'Oh, yes, fine.' She caught on and

started to eat again.

'What's this?' Chad prodded at a crispy, golden-brown puffed object on his plate and Maggie grinned.

'It's a Yorkshire pudding and traditionally served with roast beef. It's made with a batter, rather like pancakes.'

He took a bite and was relieved to find it light and delicious so it didn't have to join Scotch eggs on his list of British foods to be avoided. 'It's good.' Maggie launched into a long explanation about its origins, describing how in Yorkshire it would be baked in a large tin instead of individual servings.

'You'd get a square of pudding served with gravy before the meal, it was supposed to fill people up when there wasn't much beef to go around.'

'Makes sense. Southern cornbread served pretty much the same purpose I'm guessin'.' Chad glanced over to see their table neighbours had lost interest and winked at Maggie. 'I think we're safe,' he whispered.

They chatted happily and finished their meals.

'Dessert? Or should I say pudding?' he teased.

'You can call it what you like but I don't want any, thanks,' Maggie insisted. 'That was delicious but I'm stuffed.'

He appreciated the fact she'd enjoyed her food and had answered his question honestly. 'Me too. I'll ask about coffee.'

Ten minutes later they'd retreated to a quiet corner of the pretty garden, well away from the wooden picnic tables full of families enjoying the warm summer day. Chad sat back and let Maggie pour their drinks before he said anything.

'Tell me about Emily.'

Maggie's eyes widened. 'Goodness. I don't know where to start.'

'The beginning? It's usually the best place.'

'Right, well here goes.' She attempted to smile but it didn't reach her worried eyes.

Chad listened. He was an expert at

that, but having to sit still and hear about the burdens placed on this lovely woman was still tough. She'd been steered into becoming responsible for her sister as a child and although they were now adults the two women kept to their same assigned roles. Maggie told him everything about her conversation with her sister the previous day before she ran out of steam, going very quiet and staring off into the distance.

'I don't know either of you well, so take what I say with a pinch of salt, but I'm guessin' she's starting to question the way things are between you as much as you are.'

Maggie sighed. 'We've been this way for all our lives. I'm sure neither of us would know where to begin making changes.'

He only hesitated for a second. If things were normal and he'd met Maggie in Nashville he could've taken his time but Chad's normal way of going on hadn't worked well with other women so maybe it was time to change things up. 'It sounds as though Emily's making a start already. I totally get why the idea freaks you out.'

'No, you don't, so please don't say so just to come across as sympathetic.'

Chad ignored her and ploughed on. 'My only brother, Josh, is ten years older so we were never close as kids. We didn't argue or fight but just drifted apart and now don't seem to have anything in common.'

'How do you know if you never see him? I'm sure you've changed since you were a child and he must've done too.' She pinned him down in one moment.

'He came home for a visit after leaving the army last year, but we didn't talk much.' *Understatement.* 'He moved out to Colorado, bought a few acres of land and doesn't see anyone much,' Chad muttered, staring at a knot in the table instead of meeting Maggie's far too perceptive gaze.

'He sounds like a man in need of a good brother.' Her quiet, precise words struck at his core and Chad swallowed down the painful emotions tightening his throat. 'Perhaps you should go and visit him whether he invites you or not?'

'Yeah. I'd pretty much decided to do that when I get back. Recently I've done a lot of thinking about Josh and a ton of other stuff.' He picked up her hand, needing the reassuring contact. 'I'm not always the man you see now, Maggie.' She raised her eyebrows but didn't comment. 'Back in Nashville I've got a reputation as a hard-working, hard-partying bachelor who's determined to stay that way. My last girlfriend told me I was a flash, selfish bastard — too charming and handsome for my own good.'

'Are you warning me off?'

'Isn't that what you're trying to do to me?' He tossed the question right back at her, hating himself for using a legal tactic to avoid flaying himself wide open. Maggie was digging into places he preferred to keep locked up tight.

A flash of anger slid across her face

and Chad knew if he didn't take a leap of faith right now she was going to walk out. 'I'm sorry. That was crass. I'm not good at this.' With a wry smile he gestured at them both.

'Nor am I,' Maggie admitted. 'It's probably why we're both considered Reject Table people in the first place.'

Chad burst out laughing. 'You're great for my self-image I must say,' he jibed, 'there's no danger of ever getting an over-inflated ego around you. And I mean that in the best possible way before you get offended.' She grinned right back at him, a wide glorious smile that sent a flash of desire zinging right through him.

Maggie glanced at her wristwatch and frowned. 'I hate to say this, but I need to go and check on Emily.'

'Don't apologise. The best thing is that you said you hate the idea of leaving, so it's all good.'

He ached to kiss her until they both forgot everything else. *Timing. Chad. Timing. It's lousy. Give the woman a break*. 'Is there anything I can do to help?'

She gave a shy smile and shook her head. 'You've no idea how much you've done already.'

Tell me. Chad yearned to pin her down and ask exactly what she meant but sensed she'd already gone further than she'd intended. Frightening her off was the last thing he wanted to do. 'I'll take you home.'

This time the silence between them as they left was comfortable and easy. Maggie rested her head against his shoulder as he drove as slowly as possible until they reached her house. He parked outside and she didn't object when Chad got out to walk in with her.

Suddenly the front door opened and a black plastic bag flew out, bursting open as it landed at Chad's feet and spilling men's clothes all over the path.

'Get out, and stay gone this time,' Emily shrieked, pummelling on a well-dressed, blond-haired man who was struggling to hold onto her.

'Oh, God, it's Jonathan. Now it's going to be World War Three,' Maggie groaned.

13

Maggie strode briskly up the path. 'Get inside now, both of you, we're not arguing out on the doorstep.'

'But, Maggie, you don't know what he said . . . '

'I don't care, Ems, do what I say right now.'

Emily wriggled out of Jonathan's grasp and stomped into the house.

'I'm sorry, but it is my . . . '

She pinned Jonathan with her fiercest glare. 'You too. Inside. Now.' Maggie glanced over her shoulder and caught Chad stifling a grin. 'I could do with some moral support so you might as well come too.' She gestured towards the clothes and rubbish bag. 'Bring all that.'

'Yes, ma'am.' His mischievous smile almost cracked her attempt at being stern but she managed to hold it together.

Everyone bundled into the kitchen and Emily immediately sat down and slumped over the table with a petulant expression. Jonathan propped himself up by the sink and folded his arms across his chest.

'This is our private business. Who's he?' Jonathan asked, pointing at Chad.

'A stray Yank my dear sister picked up at a wedding yesterday,' Emily replied with a nasty smirk.

'Apologise right now.' Maggie's blood boiled over. 'I don't care how bad you're feeling or what problems you've got there's no excuse for being rude. You should be very grateful to Chad for helping us out with the cake. He saved us from looking like a pair of fools.' She grabbed hold of his hand and tilted her chin up in the air. 'Plus I happen to like him very much. More than like. So there.' A surge of embarrassed heat flooded her face.

The sucker punch caught Chad right in the gut and he struggled to keep his wits about him. He stuck out his other hand. 'Chad Robertson.' Jonathan gingerly took it and gave them both a bemused look. 'Music attorney from Nashville, Tennessee.' He gave Maggie a big wink. 'Equally smitten with this lovely lady.' Chad bent down and kissed her, right on the mouth.

Oh, heck. She knew he'd taste delicious, but . . .

'For goodness sake, Maggie.' Emily's disgust was obvious. 'I'm pregnant and have been deserted by my baby's father, and all you can do is throw yourself at some man you haven't known for five minutes.'

'It's about twenty-seven hours if we're splitting hairs,' Chad observed.

'I didn't desert you either, well, not exactly.' Jonathan stammered. 'I mean, I didn't know you were . . . '

'Shut up, all of you,' Maggie yelled. The room fell silent and three pairs of eyes stared at her in bemusement. 'All of this upset isn't doing Emily and the baby any good. I'm going to make a pot of tea and we'll talk this over sensibly.'

Before Emily could do any more than open her mouth Maggie scowled and her sister shut up.

'Well done,' Chad whispered in her ear and the admiration in his voice gave her a bolt of much needed courage.

When everyone had their tea Maggie sat next to Emily. 'First I want to hear what Jonathan has to say.'

'But he . . . '

'Thanks, Maggie.' He shifted from one foot to the other then paced around the room, looking anywhere but at her sister. 'I love Emily. Always have done.' Jonathan hesitated. 'But she can be a bit . . . difficult at times.'

'Tell them what you did,' Emily blurted out.

'She pushed me to set a wedding date and I wasn't sure we were ready.'

'*I* was.' She protested.

He came over to kneel on the floor next to her side and picked up her hands. 'No, you weren't, Emily. We've been having some issues and you know it but you were scared of losing me. I told you that wouldn't happen.'

'But it did.'

'I couldn't handle your erratic outbursts anymore.'

Emily paled. 'So you went to a party, got drunk and slept with a tart.'

'It wasn't like that.' Jonathan protested.

Maggie could see at this rate they'd be there until midnight and no further ahead. Succinctly she rattled off all the things Emily accused him of and asked if he'd done each one. He quickly said yes to the first two, but then went quiet.

'Hey, pal, get it over with, you're not helping yourself here,' Chad interjected.

'I wasn't unfaithful to Emily. I couldn't be. It would kill me,' Jonathan protested.

'But you told me you did,' Emily said calmly. 'Why did you lie?'

'Because it was the worst thing he could think of.' Chad took a chance and spoke up. 'We men are idiots sometimes. Take pity on him, kid, and listen to what he's *really* saying.' He caught Maggie's sharp intake of breath and knew she was waiting for her sister to go into tantrum mode again.

Emily sat up very straight. 'Jonathan, we need to talk on our own.' She glanced over at them. 'No offence, you two.'

'None taken,' Chad said and slipped his arm around Maggie's shoulder. 'How about you and I go for a walk?'

'A walk? But . . . '

'They'll be fine.' He stared deep into her worried eyes, trying to convey his belief that it was time to let Emily deal with her own problems. 'Do you want to change into something more comfortable? We can stop by the pub for me to do the same on the way.'

'I suppose we could.' Maggie's reluctance couldn't have been more obvious if she'd spelled it out in flashing neon lights. 'Are you absolutely sure?' She asked Emily.

'Yes. I promise not to yell, hit Jonathan or burst into tears. Okay?'

Maggie sighed and nodded. Without saying any more she left the room and disappeared upstairs.

Chad considered going outside to wait, not wanting to make things more awkward than they already were.

'Thanks, mate.' Jonathan pulled out the chair next to Emily and sat down. 'I bet you're good at your job.' He gave Chad a wry smile.

'Most of the time.'

'If you mess my sister around you'll have me to deal with,' Emily threatened before giving in to a tight smile. 'You've witnessed me when I'm angry so that should be your warning.'

'It certainly is,' he jokingly agreed.

Maggie reappeared in the kitchen door and stared around at them all laughing, obviously convinced they were completely mad.

'Everything's fine. Off we go.' Without giving her a chance to argue he seized her hand and whisked her outside. He had her settled in his car before she had a chance to protest.

'You're very domineering sometimes,' Maggie groused without any real venom.

'I prefer to call it decisive.'

'Hmm. You would.'

He grinned and started up the engine, putting the car in gear and driving away before Maggie could change her mind and insist they go back inside to referee. 'I love your hair loose.' She'd left it undone today and the dark brown waves rippled around her face.

'It's a mess, but I have to tie it back for cooking so I usually don't bother when I'm free from work.' She shrugged. 'I'm envious of yours.'

'Mine?'

She nodded and stared down at her knees.

Chad tried not to give in to a satisfied smile. 'We'll discuss this when I'm not trying to concentrate on staying on the right side of the road — or rather the left.'

A few minutes later they were back at

the Black Prince where things were quieter now the lunch-time rush was over. He pulled into a parking spot close to the front door. 'How about you go and sit in the public lounge while I throw on some jeans?'

'I'd prefer to wait for you in the garden if you don't mind. It's too pretty a day to be inside.' Maggie insisted and left before he could argue.

Chad hummed to himself as he took the stairs two at a time. He hoped he wasn't reading too much into her confusion around him because he felt exactly the same way. Fumbling with his door key he let himself into the room. As fast as he could Chad kicked off his black dress shoes and quickly stripped off the shirt and khaki trousers he'd worn for lunch. He pulled on his old jeans, a dark green T-shirt and trainers and was ready to go.

He ran back down and hurried out into the garden.

'There you are. Tonya's here for your date.' Maggie's sharp tone of voice

chilled him. She wasn't smiling anymore.

'Date?' His gaze rested on his Reject
Table nemesis, wearing another tight
fitting dress, this one bright yellow with
a neckline that plunged down to her
waist.

Tonya gave a complacent smile. 'I
was telling dear Maggie that I'd come
over to start showing you around
Cornwall. I couldn't let you go alone.
We'll start with Land's End this
afternoon.' She took a step closer and
trailed her glossy red fingernails down
his bare arm. Chad jerked away and
wrapped his arm around Maggie's stiff
shoulders.

'Thanks, but I've already made other
plans, Tonya.'

Her green eyes narrowed. 'We had a
little misunderstanding yesterday but
things are different now, aren't they
Maggie?'

'What's going on?' he murmured to
Maggie but she pulled away from his
grasp.

'I need to go back home.' Her voice broke. 'I'll leave you two alone to get on with your sightseeing.' She took off running across the grass and Chad's fury erupted.

He seized Tonya's arm. 'What the hell did you say to her?'

'Only the truth.'

'You're a deeply unpleasant woman,' he hissed. 'I'm going after Maggie.' Chad strode off.

'When you catch up with her ask what she did to rip her family apart,' Tonya yelled, but he didn't turn around.

14

Maggie raced out through the pub, ignoring the stares she received from the few customers lingering by the bar, and hurled herself out of the front door. Halfway across the car park she stumbled on the rough gravel. From nowhere a strong hand grabbed her wrist and saved her from falling.

'Are you alright?' Chad's concern tore at her and Maggie couldn't fight any longer when he wrapped his arms around her. She allowed her head to rest on his firm chest and savoured the reassuring thump of his heartbeat. 'I've no idea what all that was about but you're going to tell me and we'll sort it out. I hope you know me better than to believe I made any sort of arrangement with her?'

She couldn't lie. 'Of course I don't.' Maggie hesitated. 'But I hate the idea of spoiling your good opinion of me.'

Chad eased back so she was forced to look up at him. 'Don't jump to conclusions. I told you *I'm* not perfect and *you're* still here.'

If only it was that simple.

'Don't take this the wrong way, honey, but we need somewhere quiet to talk. How about we go up to my room?'

Despite everything she had to bite her lip to stop from laughing. Finally a gorgeous man invites her into his bedroom but all he wants to do is talk. Maggie allowed him to lead her back inside the pub and they headed up the dark staircase without speaking. He unlocked the first door they came to along the narrow hallway.

'Welcome to my humble abode.' Chad walked in first, hastily scooping up clothes from the floor and tossing them in a heap in the corner of the room.

Maggie glanced awkwardly around, her eyes drawn to the large bed with its garish floral bedspread and mound of lacy pillows.

'Tasteful, isn't it?' He smiled and gestured towards a plush red velvet armchair over by the small bay window. Chad toed off his shoes and stretched out on the bed, plumped up the pillows and rested his hands behind his head.

She ignored the chair and stood in front of him. She'd get this over with quickly — like ripping off a plaster. 'Did Tonya say anything about me after I left?' He didn't answer right away and her heart clenched. *Enough said.*

'Yeah. She told me to ask what you did to rip your family apart. I guessed she was simply being her usual annoying self. Do you want to join me?' Chad's eyes gleamed as he patted the bed. 'Only if it'll make things easier for you of course.'

'You're so noble.' She played along and the knot of tension in the pit of her stomach eased its grip. Maggie slipped off her own shoes and perched on the edge of the bed.

'I won't bite.' Chad bared his white teeth, 'I promised Great Aunt Audrey.'

He reached over to cover her hand with his own and the comforting touch of his warm skin helped. 'Do you remember when Emily was rude to me yesterday and you said I didn't deserve being spoken to that way?'

'Sure do.'

'I had my reasons for disagreeing with you, I wasn't simply being weird. When I was sixteen I went to a friend's party after my parents told me not to.'

Chad pulled her gently down to lie with him and wrapped his arms around her, his clean scent both soothing and arousing her at the same time. 'It's okay. I'm here. Nothing bad is going to happen to you.'

Yes, it is, you're going to hate me and I can't bear it.

★ ★ ★

'Tell me what happened.' He'd been to enough unauthorised parties to know

142

there must be more to Maggie's story. Chad stroked her hair, playing idly with the silky curls and she softened into him. He steeled his body not to react to her nearness, but a light sweat formed on his forehead with the effort. *You should've found a quiet spot in the lounge to talk, you idiot.*

'Emily wasn't invited but she followed me there. I was sick of her always spoiling everything for me and I told her exactly what I thought of her. I told her to go back home.' Maggie stammered and buried her head in his chest to avoid meeting his questioning eyes. 'She got mad at me and then rang our mother to come and pick her up. Of course Mum came right away because all my sister ever had to do was click her fingers. Emily spotted her parked outside and ran into the street,' Maggie gulped. 'My sweet mother saw a car driving towards them and pushed Emily out of the way.'

'But your mother was hit?' He

ventured. Maggie's shuddering sobs ran through him and Chad clutched her tighter.

'Head on. She died a week later.'

'Aw, honey, I'm sorry.'

'Afterwards my Dad made it clear that continuing to look out for Emily was the least I could do. He passed away five years ago — they claimed it was complications from pneumonia but I think it was a broken heart . . . ' Her voice faltered.

Chad brushed away the slow trickle of tears rolling down her cheeks. 'Have you and Emily talked about all this?'

'We don't need to.' She shook her head. 'She's always made it clear I was to blame.'

'That's not fair.'

Maggie jerked out of his arms. 'You don't understand. Nobody can.'

He needed to tread carefully if she wasn't to freak out at him. 'Answer me one thing. If this had happened the other way around would you still hold this over Emily's head?'

Deep frown lines creased her forehead and after several long painfully silent moments she half-heartedly shrugged.

'I didn't think so.'

'But she's . . . '

Chad rested his fingers gently on her trembling hand. 'Different? Not in any insurmountable sense.'

'It's not that simple,' she yelled and burst into tears.

'Let it all out, Maggie.' Chad gathered her back into his arms. 'It's fine, you don't have to be tough all the time. Not any more.' She glanced up at him, her blue eyes shining, and Chad cradled her face in his hands.

He pressed a soft kiss on Maggie's lush mouth and her contented sigh encouraged him to deepen the kiss. Surrounded by her luscious vanilla scent Chad slipped one hand down to press against the base of her spine and ease her closer.

She's worth more than this. You're taking advantage.

Sometimes he hated his overactive conscience. Chad sucked in a deep breath, gritted his teeth and pulled away.

'Why did you stop?' Hurt ran through Maggie's voice. 'Was it so terrible you couldn't bear to go on kissing me?'

'No, sweetheart, far from it. That kiss was too damn good and I'm not made of stone.'

'I noticed,' she murmured, looking embarrassed.

'I can't take advantage of you while you're upset.'

A mischievous smile crept across her mouth. 'So when I'm not upset it'll be okay?'

'Hey, now who's twisting whose words?' he retorted. 'I'm trying to be a gentleman. I told you what my reputation is in Nashville, but I don't want to be that man with you. You're special.'

'Oh.' Maggie's sultry gaze swept down over him and reignited the fierce desire he'd managed to dampen down a few seconds ago. At a guess he'd say she'd never experienced this level of power over a man before and liked it, a lot.

'You're one wicked lady,' he chuckled.

'What a thing to say.' Her protest was patently fake and they both laughed. 'Maybe the original walk we'd planned would cool us down?'

'A very sensible idea.' Reluctantly he moved to the edge of the bed and found his shoes.

'Being sensible sucks,' she complained. 'One day I'm going to do exactly what I want with no thought to the consequences.'

'Oh, Maggie, you could no more do that than Emily could turn into a completely responsible person with a placid disposition,' he tossed right back at her. 'Get real.'

She stuck out her tongue and turned her back on him. A noise like a clanging ship's bell hummed somewhere in the room and Maggie jumped up to grab her handbag from the floor. She pulled out her phone and glanced at the screen before answering. 'Emily. How are things?' The smile left her face.

Chad crossed his fingers. He'd backed up Maggie's sister when she'd insisted they leave her alone with Jonathan. Had he made a huge mistake?

15

Maggie listened in amazement and prayed Emily wasn't making another rash decision. 'Are you absolutely sure?' She held the phone away from her ear to avoid being deafened — catching the words insensitive, boring and true love. 'Okay, okay, I'll come back right now. Bye.' She turned back to face Chad who was looking more worried than she'd ever seen him. 'Don't panic. Jonathan isn't lying in a pool of blood on my kitchen floor.'

'Good.' His succinct reply made her smile. 'What happened?'

'Don't ask me how but the engagement is back on and tomorrow morning they're going to the registry office and fill in the paperwork to get married in sixteen days.'

Chad glanced at the calendar on his phone. 'Is the fifth of August significant in some way?'

Maggie shrugged. 'Apparently the notice of an intended marriage has to be displayed for fifteen days before the ceremony so it's the earliest possible date.' He opened his mouth to speak but she jumped in first. 'Yes, I know what Jonathan said but I suppose impending fatherhood combined with Emily's charms persuaded him otherwise. His parents won't be pleased because they consider my sister to be nothing but trouble.' Chad held out his hand and she let herself be pulled back into his arms. She'd never realised before how strong and reassuring a hug could be and snuggled into him, as close as it was possible to get with their clothes on. *Stop thinking about that, Maggie Taylor, or you'll never leave this room.*

'Would you like me to take you home?' he murmured, kissing his way down her neck. 'You're so hot, Maggie Taylor, you should come with a health warning.'

'I'll have you know my kitchens have

always scored top marks in inspections. My potentially hazardous foods are properly thawed. I maintain good hygiene practises and all handling of food is minimised.'

'What a relief,' he teased. 'Let's go before I lose the will to say no to you about anything.'

Maggie tried not to look incredibly satisfied but didn't succeed judging by the gleam in Chad's eyes, turning them a rich shade of dark, decadent toffee. She found her shoes and slipped them back on before gathering up her handbag. Folding her hands demurely she waited for him to get ready.

'Don't give me that fake innocent look as though butter wouldn't melt in your mouth.' Chad waved his keys in the air. 'Downstairs. Now.'

She obeyed without saying another word, enjoying the fact the light-hearted flirtation had briefly taken her mind off Emily. She should do it more often.

What was it with her and sitting alone in the kitchen? Somehow it always helped after a challenging day and this one certainly ranked up there with the most difficult she'd experienced. She stared at the clock and was surprised to see it was nearly midnight. In her heart she wanted to be happy for Emily, but the nagging sensation of impending doom wouldn't go away. Chad had made it all sound perfectly rational but the man was a lawyer and everyone knew they could convince other people black was white with the right choice of words. Maybe she wasn't being fair to him because he dealt with music rights day in and day out not defending murderous criminals.

We've got it all planned, Maggie. It'll be an intimate ceremony with only our immediate families. Afterwards I'll move into Jonathan's flat in town until we find a house to buy. You'll be able to have this place to yourself.

Maggie couldn't imagine rattling around in their old family home alone, plus legally it belonged to them both and should be sold to give Emily her share.

I'll stay in the business, but I'm not sure how much work I'll be able to put in so you may need to get someone else to help out.

It'd taken all her waning self-control to hold back from screaming at that point. She hadn't wanted to open a catering business in the first place. Cakes were her real love. They'd have to talk about it more when Emily's head wasn't full of flower colours and whether the dress she'd bought was suitable for a registry office wedding.

Jonathan had whisked Emily off out for a celebratory dinner but Maggie pleaded a non-existent headache when Chad tried hard to persuade her to go out with him. Now she wished she wasn't here alone with her thoughts.

The clock chimed the hour and she realised it was Monday meaning her bizarre weekend was officially over. Maggie sighed and decided she'd better drag herself up to her empty Chad-less bed.

The sheets were tangled uncomfortably around his legs and Chad threw off the covers before turning the bedside light back on. He didn't do restless well. When he went to bed he slept, but the combination of craving Maggie and knowing he'd said all the wrong things earlier had kept him wide awake. He picked up his phone and tapped in a text message before hitting Send. No doubt she was fast asleep but at least when she read it in the morning Maggie would know he'd been thinking about her. A couple of seconds later a reply came back.

I'll put the kettle on. Emily went to stay with Jonathan. The house is empty without her.

And lonely. He heard her unspoken words. Chad jumped out of bed with a grin plastered all over his face. He threw his clothes back on and sneaked downstairs and out to his car, driving off quietly to avoid rousing anyone in the pub.

He tapped on the front door with his stomach churning like a teenage boy on his first date. Maggie opened it immediately and Chad's body zoomed into overdrive. *Oh, hell, Maggie. Baby blue short pyjamas? Really? Your legs are seriously gorgeous and you smell so hot, sweet and wonderful I want to eat you up. Have some pity on me.*

'Thanks for coming.' She raised up on her tiptoes and brushed her lips against his stubble-roughened cheek. The tremor running through him didn't have anything to do with the cool night air.

'You invited me.'

'Neither of us were sleeping. It made sense.' The tinge of colour making her cheeks glow said what he knew she couldn't — this was far more than a simple case of insomnia. 'Tea or coffee?'

'Coffee, please.'

155

'It's only instant.'

I don't care if it's sawdust shavings off the floor. 'Doesn't matter.' Her eyes widened in surprise at his gruff reply. Chad considered apologising but came to a swift decision that shutting up was his best option. He followed her into the kitchen and sat down.

'You weren't the problem earlier, it was me,' Maggie blurted out. 'You were being rational but I didn't want to listen.'

'Emily's your sister and you love her. You've protected her all your life for a multitude of reasons.' Chad pulled her down onto his lap. She held her spine as straight as a steel rod until he stroked his fingers up and down her back and she softened into his touch. 'Maybe it's time to let go,' he murmured and dragged his lips over her velvety skin. 'You'll still be there for her.'

'But what if it all goes wrong? What if having a baby makes her worse? What if . . .'

He kissed her, gently at first but

when she responded with unabashed fervour Chad gave up on holding back. Shoving his hands up through her silky hair he pulled her closer and little pleasured noises escaped the back of Maggie's throat. He deepened the kiss further and groaned when she ran her fingers over his chest and tugged at the hem of his T-shirt.

'Maggie, you were discussing Emily. I thought you wanted to talk it through.' He choked out the words but she only laughed and carried on exploring under his shirt. Her caressing fingers heated his bare skin and made him shudder.

'Maybe I don't want to anymore.'

Chad forced himself to ease away and seize hold of her hands to stop her teasing explorations. 'Are you absolutely sure? I don't want you to regret . . . '

'Do you want to make love to me or don't you?' Maggie challenged, her sapphire eyes flashing.

'I really do.' Chad's raspy voice betrayed him and a satisfied smile crept across her face. 'How about we take this upstairs?' Maggie nodded and slid off his lap. She held out her hand and he took it, letting her lead the way.

At the top of the stairs she opened her bedroom door and glancing back over her shoulder at him, a shadow of uncertainty darkened her eyes.

'You're free to change your mind,' Chad offered, desperately hoping she wouldn't. 'It's okay. I'll never do anything you don't want me to. Ever.'

'I know that, or you wouldn't be here.' Maggie opened her arms to him. 'Hold me. Please.'

He eased her into his embrace, sensing her tremble.

'I need to tell you something,' she whispered, 'I haven't done this for a very long time . . . I was a teenager and it was only once — a drunken fumble in the back of a car . . . I'm not sure I'll be very good . . . '

Chad silenced her with a long, hard kiss before pulling away. 'If that's anything to go by being 'good' won't be an issue, honey. Don't fret. We'll take as long as you want.' He kissed her again, taking his time and waiting until she begged for more before taking the next step. Sometimes talking was overrated.

16

Maggie stretched out in the bed and opened her eyes, blinking against the bright sunlight streaming in. She couldn't remember drawing her bedroom curtains last night.

'Good mornin'.' Chad's delicious drawl insinuated into her brain and everything came flooding back. She glanced over to see him lying next to her; naked, gorgeous and smiling at her as though he'd won the lottery.

You don't do pick-ups at weddings. It's undignified and desperate. Maggie groaned.

Chad's brow furrowed. 'You promised me you wouldn't regret this . . . us.'

'It's not that exactly,' she stammered, 'but I don't usually get carried away. This might be normal for you, but . . . '

'Thanks a bunch.' He sat up and she

couldn't avoid staring at every inch of his tanned, broad chest only inches away from her fascinated gaze. Maggie's face heated remembering the breathtaking way he'd loved her all last night and again when they'd turned to each other as dawn was breaking. 'In case you're interested I don't make a habit of going to weddings and hooking up with another reject simply to pass the time,' Chad snapped and jumped out of the bed, grabbing his clothes off the floor.

'I didn't mean it that way.'

'Then what *did* you mean?'

This must be how a witness felt being cross-examined in court. 'I'm sorry. Sit down, please.' She patted the bed. 'You're intimidating me.' Chad's stony face softened and he dropped back down on the crumpled bedcovers.

'That wasn't my intention, but . . . '

She reached over and touched his hand. 'I've hurt your feelings and I couldn't be sorrier.' A flood of embarrassed heat lit up her face and neck.

'I've never woken up with a man before and I don't know how I'm supposed to behave.' Tears pricked at her eyes and he leaned in to kiss her mouth, rubbing his thumb down over her cheek.

'You're not *supposed* to do anything. Just be the same sweet, honest woman you were before we made love. That's all I need,' Chad murmured, 'can you do that?' His plea struck a direct path to her heart and Maggie nodded. 'You wanna start the morning again?'

She smiled shyly and he eased her back on the bed, surrounding her with his warm musky scent. Wrapping her in his strong arms he started to love her all over again and every one of Maggie's thoughts about what was proper or sensible fled.

* * *

His fingers played with Maggie's soft hair spread over the pillow but Chad's mind raced as he watched her sleep. How would she react if he suggested staying in Cornwall longer? He couldn't say goodbye, get on a plane back to Nashville and chalk this up as a quick fling. Maggie had turned his life around in a few short days and he needed to try and make sense of it somehow. The fact that he had an active social life back home and had so far avoided commitment had led to his reputation as a carefree bachelor with no desire to change. His grandmother gave him a lecture the day before he came.

Use this vacation as a chance to take some time out, Chandler. Playing the field is all very well for a young man, but you're old enough to start thinking more about the future. Your father won't come out and say so but I know he'd like to take things easier. He's been hoping you'd decide to give up the law and take over running the firm. Josh needs our help as well but he's too stubborn to ask for it. You could do a lot for him if you chose to.

He'd almost protested that he had no interest in running the family's guitar business, but it would've been a lie and his grandmother would soon have caught him out. The idea of working on the designs and marketing for the top-end guitars his family had made for three generations intrigued him but until now he'd avoided it out of sheer wilfulness on his part. Maybe he'd finally grown up. As for Josh, he didn't need his grandmother to prod him on that score. She'd be pleased to find out he'd emailed his brother last night and promised to come to Colorado soon for a visit. He hadn't stopped to ask if he'd be welcome and guessed he'd find out when he got there.

'You look thoughtful,' Maggie murmured, rolling over to snuggle into him. She gazed up at him with her soft, deep blue eyes full of warmth and caring. 'Spit it out.'

He'd forced her to be honest and it was his turn to do the same. 'I might scare you off.' Maggie's face creased into a wide smile.

'I don't scare easily.'

You might if I tell you I'm pretty sure I've found the woman I want to marry and it's you. 'Good.' Chad trailed gentle kisses down her neck, nipping at her smooth skin and doing his best to distract her from serious conversation.

Maggie firmly pushed him away. 'Honesty. Remember?'

'Yeah, I know,' he sighed, psyching himself up to receive his marching orders. He'd start by admitting he was considering staying a few extra days and see how that went before going any further. Chad ploughed on and watched her eyes widen in surprise. *Good one. She'll never believe the rest.*

'You don't have to stay out of some misguided sense of guilt because we've slept together.' She stumbled over her words. 'Stop grinning.' Maggie smacked his arm.

'You're so damn beautiful when you blush and then get mad at yourself.'

She opened and closed her mouth several times without uttering a sound.

'Trust me I'm not suggesting staying

out of guilt because I have none.'

'Oh.' A tiny smile tugged at Maggie's mouth.

'The thing is I've found out something in the last forty-eight hours and if it doesn't scare you, it sure as heck scares me,' Chad admitted and his cheeks burned. 'You've turned my life upside down and inside out Maggie Taylor.'

'And?'

He might as well get it over with because she was one determined woman and would nag him until he broke down and told her the truth. 'Fine, here goes.' Chad's heart thumped so hard he was afraid it'd burst through his chest. 'I'm think I've found the woman I want to marry and it's you.'

'You're asking me to marry you?' she shrieked.

'No, I didn't say that,' Chad blurted, 'well, not exactly, I mean . . . ' How had he got himself tangled up in knots? *You met the woman staring at you as if you're completely mad. She's made you that way.* He seized her hands. 'What I mean is I think I'm in love with you, but I know it's too soon. I'm probably crazy and you'd never even consider it.' Chad swallowed hard. 'You *made* me say it, Maggie.'

'Now it's my fault you sort of proposed while not really meaning to?' she challenged and Chad groaned.

'Oh, heck, this isn't how I wanted it to come out.' He shoved his hands through his hair.

'Don't do that,' she hissed, glaring at him.

'What?'

'That thing with your hair,' Maggie muttered under her breath.

God, what was she talking about now?

'You do it all the time. Push your hands through your hair and then it falls back into place, except one bit always flops forward. It's so thick and glossy and . . . ' Her voice trailed away and he almost felt sorry for her.

No you don't, not really, you get a kick out of it.

'Right,' he dragged out the single word and fought against smirking.

'Back to the subject in hand.' Maggie pulled up the sheet to cover herself, giving him a stern glare. 'I'll answer as honestly as I can. I have a sneaking suspicion I love you as well but as you say it's too soon. I'm probably equally crazy and all I'm saying for now is that I *might* consider your 'suggestion' at some point.'

'Okay.' Chad thought he'd just been sort-of accepted. Maybe. 'You want to leave it there for now?'

'Well I'm hardly going to suggest going to the nearest jewellery shop, am I?' Maggie's sharp sense of humour re-emerged and he relaxed again. 'You'd better get dressed and clear out of here before my dear sister puts in an appearance. I am not ready to explain any of this to her.' She gestured at them both and the bed. 'You can return at half past two showered, well-dressed and ready for us to brave Great Aunt Audrey in her lair.'

'Yes, ma'am.' Chad popped a quick kiss on her lush, tempting lips. 'Will I need a bulletproof vest?'

Maggie's eyebrows raised. 'Hardly, although you might consider a bunch of flowers. She'll say they're a waste of money but if you don't take any you'll be marked down as cheap.'

'She already thinks I'm a crass, mouthy Yank so it'd only be one more black mark against me.'

'Great Aunt Audrey is one smart woman,' she joked and poked his arm. 'I need to hurry into the kitchen and bake a coffee and walnut sponge. It's her favourite although she'll complain about that too — it won't be the right size, it'll be too sweet and have either too much or not enough icing. But that's alright. It's her way and I know she loves me really.'

Chad cupped his hand behind her neck and eased her towards him for a last kiss. 'That's all that matters.' It took all his self-control to stop and pull away. 'I'd better go.'

'Mm. I suppose you had,' Maggie sighed.

Reluctantly he got back up from the bed and dressed, not daring to look at her again until he was ready. 'You gonna come down and kiss me goodbye?' Chad said hopefully.

'If you're good.'

'You mean I wasn't good enough already?' he teased, pretending to be offended. 'Maybe I'll have to come back tonight and try harder.'

'You are so wicked.' Maggie wagged her finger playfully in his face. 'Anyway that depends on Emily.'

'Fair enough.'

They headed downstairs and Chad managed to sneak in several more kisses before she made him leave. Now it was time to get prepared to win over the old lady. If he could get her firmly on his side Maggie would be next.

17

'This is it?' Chad's voice rose and Maggie stifled a giggle.

Holland House always surprised people the first time they saw the magnificent white rendered Art Deco era building. No doubt Chad imagined Audrey lived in a sprawling, gloomy old mansion run by a couple of ancient family retainers. 'It isn't what you expected?'

'You know it's not,' Chad retorted. 'You could've warned me.'

'And what fun would that have been?' She laughed as he mumbled complaints about weird English women under his breath. 'Park anywhere along the front. Audrey owns the whole house but only lives on the top floor since she was widowed and rents out the downstairs.'

Chad stopped the car and quickly

walked around to open Maggie's door. He took the cake box from her hands while she got out before passing it back to her. Reaching into the car he took out a stunning bouquet of cream lilies. He locked up the car and stood still for a moment, scrutinising her godmother's home.

'A lot of people believe this house inspired the designer of the Tate Gallery here in St. Ives,' Maggie explained, pointing to the sprawling town spread out beneath their view. Clinging to the edge of the water it shimmered in the afternoon sunshine making it obvious why so many artists had been drawn here over the years. 'I'd tell you more but that would spoil Audrey's moment of glory.' She remembered being brought here as a small child by her mother and warned to be on her best behaviour. But Audrey had let her touch anything she wanted as long as she was careful and told her the fascinating stories behind every piece of furniture and the myriad of paintings and sculptures.

'We wouldn't want that. She's going to enjoy crowing over me. I mentioned my interest in early twentieth century English design but she didn't say anything about owning this little gem.' Chad chuckled. 'I may, or may not mention my own family's pre-Civil War mansion. Depends how much she gloats.'

Maggie laughed along with him, but a sliver of uneasiness ran through her.

'Hey, honey, it's just a house. It's nothing to do with us.' He slid his arm around her shoulder.

She wanted to be reassured but knew it had *everything* to do with them. This wasn't real life for either of them. It didn't matter whether it happened in three days or three weeks, at some point the fantasy would blow up and they'd be faced with the truth.

Gently he turned her to face him. 'Don't create obstacles. Be open to new possibilities.'

'You sound like a fortune cookie,' she jibed.

'If you weren't guarding that cake with your life I'd kiss you senseless to stop the nonsense you're spouting. But sadly it'd only give Audrey looking down on us from her vantage point more ammunition.'

'Do you think she's watching?'

'Yep, I'd bet anything on it and if we're even thirty seconds late I'll get the blame.' He grinned and brandished the flowers like a weapon. 'Come on. Let's go and have tea.'

'Right.' With a resigned sigh Maggie led the way. She opened the front door and stepped into the massive rectangular entrance hall.

'Very dramatic. The architect knew how to make a stunning first impression.' Chad's dry comment made her smile.

Maggie loved the dark green and white geometric tiles, stained glass windows and sweeping wrought-iron staircase, always imagining herself arriving here ready for a glamorous cocktail party. 'We could take the lift but I'm sure Audrey would prefer us to walk. You'll get an amazing view over the beach and the town plus appreciate the design of the house far better.'

I also get to spend longer with you, always a bonus. Chad let Maggie walk on up first and followed slowly behind her. On the way he made mental notes of everything he saw, determined to come back and take pictures another day. His father wouldn't believe it unless he had proof.

'Here we are.' She gestured towards a set of stainless steel and glass doors. Chad sensed her nervousness increase and her fingers tightened around the square white cake box.

Before Maggie could touch the doorbell a young woman popped her head out around and beckoned them inside. 'Mrs Trembarth is waiting for you. I'm Louise Giles, her assistant.'

Out of the corner of his eye Chad spotted an intriguing sculpture sitting in the middle of a small oval table and couldn't resist taking a closer look.

'Do you recognise that?' Audrey's challenge rang out from the far end of the room.

'Of course. Eric Gill's Divine Lovers. 1923. Excellent copy.'

Maggie stifled a laugh and he winked to tell her they were in this together.

'Hmm. Come over where I can see you both.' Audrey beckoned to them, her silhouette framed by the distinctive radius bay windows behind her; one aspect of Art Deco style he particularly admired.

'These are for you.' Chad proffered the flowers and caught the older woman's quick flash of surprise before she gave him a slight nod. 'Louise will take them away to arrange later. Do sit down so we can have our tea and talk.'

You mean you'll talk and we'll listen.

'I made one of your favourite coffee and walnut cakes this morning,' Maggie ventured, holding out the box. She received a slight half-smile in return which he guessed indicated extreme happiness in Audrey's book.

'Thank you, dear. Louise will cut it up for us,' Audrey decreed, passing the box over.

A tea tray loaded with striking brightly coloured china was set down on the glass coffee table in front of them and Chad stared in amazement at the distinctive triangular pattern. It was probably bad manners but he picked up the nearest cup and upturned it to read the words on the bottom. He let out a low whistle. *'Hand painted Bizarre by Clarice Cliff, Newport Pottery England.'*

'Do you like it, Mr Robertson?' Audrey's sharp tone was belied by the shine lighting up her pale blue eyes.

'I sure do, ma'am.' He didn't attempt to hide his admiration. 'My father has been an avid collector for years and I'm a particular admirer of Clarice Cliff's early works. This is nineteen twenty-seven or eight I'd say. The on-glaze enamel colours are what make it so bright. I've never seen a complete set outside of a museum.'

Maggie scrutinised them both as though they'd come from another planet. He'd forgotten she knew very little about him outside of his non-existent cooking abilities and his talents in . . . other areas that he didn't dare think about right now.

'They were a wedding gift from my late husband in homage to my Clarice Cliff obsession. We'd recently inherited this house from my parents and the china was a perfect fit,' Audrey explained and turned to Maggie. 'I'm afraid your new boyfriend would prefer to drool over my Art Deco collection rather than discuss what I *really* brought you here to talk about.'

'Not at all. I'll come back another day to . . . drool, as you so delicately phrased it, if I'm invited of course,' Chad said, hoping he'd succeeded in convincing her that he wasn't an ignorant lout.

Audrey nodded. 'You'll be welcome at any time. I always enjoy sharing my love of the era with other connoisseurs.'

If it wouldn't have horrified her Chad could've kissed the old lady.

A charming smile crept over Maggie's face as she realised they'd had some quasi-royal blessing bestowed on them. Suddenly her good humour faded away and she frowned.

'What *did* you want to discuss?'

'Firstly, Emily. I heard very disturbing rumours at the wedding on Saturday. Of course they were spread by Tonya, but unfortunately she's often right where gossip is concerned.'

Chad reached over and squeezed Maggie's hand, wanting to remind her that he was on her side, in every way she wanted him to be.

She tilted her head defiantly. 'I expect you heard that Jonathan broke off their engagement. It was true at the time but they've since reconciled and Emily is behaving in a very mature, responsible way.' *For a change.* Chad was sure Audrey heard Maggie's unsaid words too. 'They're expecting a baby together and will be married on the fifth of August.' As the words tumbled out the old lady's features hardened.

Maggie tightened her hold on Chad's large, warm hand and fixed her gaze firmly on Audrey. She waited for the lecture to begin.

'It's not an ideal way to start, but maybe this will be the making of Emily. With a child to look after she won't have the time to be as self-absorbed. Hopefully her fiancé has a stern backbone or it won't last long,' Audrey expounded, giving Chad a stern side-ways glance that he interpreted as meaning he'd better have one too. 'I assume you won't keep the business going? I know she talked you into starting it in the first place.'

Maggie shifted in her seat. She hadn't made her mind up yet what to do and wasn't ready to be pinned down.

'You might say it's none of my business . . . yet,' Chad intervened, 'but

Maggie's had a lot to process this last couple of days. She doesn't need to be pushed into *anything* by *anybody* before she's ready.'

'A lot to process? How very American. In a minute you'll tell me she needs to get 'closure'. I consider Maggie to be as much a part of my family as Fiona and I frequently offer family members my opinions and advice. Whether or not they take it is completely up to them. But I will not be silent, Mr Robertson, when someone I . . . care for needs help and guidance.'

Maggie knew she'd better jump in before this disintegrated into a full-scale row. Chad wouldn't hold back out of some outdated notion of deference and he'd staunchly defend her even if it meant giving Audrey a heart attack. 'Stop, please, both of you.' They stared at her as though she was the crazy one. 'I appreciate you're trying to help but you're only making things worse. I'm going to help Emily plan her wedding and once that's over and she and

Jonathan are settled I'll make some decisions about my own life.'

'I'm sorry,' Chad hurried to apologise. 'I didn't mean you weren't capable of . . . '

She kissed him directly on the mouth, ignoring Audrey's disapproving scowl. 'I know. We'll talk later. Promise.' Maggie turned back to her elderly almost-relative. 'I know you want the best for me and if I need help I won't hesitate to ask.' She couldn't resist smiling. 'Of course you might give me another lecture, but I know it's done from the kindness of your heart so I don't mind.' *Not much anyway.* She leaned over and kissed Audrey's papery skin, causing two round red splotches of heat to colour her godmother's sunken cheeks. 'I love you.' Audrey murmured something and Maggie didn't ask her to repeat it. They didn't do overt displays of affection, and she'd already embarrassed the older woman enough.

'Drink your tea or it will get cold,'

Audrey ordered. 'Of course as I understand it you Americans prefer it that way,' she scoffed.

'We sure do, ma'am,' Chad's usually soft drawl thickened and it was all Maggie could do not to laugh out loud. 'We're partial to tossing your tea in our harbours too on occasion,' he retorted. Maggie was shocked when Audrey suddenly burst out laughing; a rich, warm sound she didn't remember ever hearing before.

'You're a very outspoken young man.'

'Thank you. My parents raised me that way.'

'When you return to Cornwall to marry Maggie you will bring them to stay here. I would enjoy picking your father's brains,' Audrey declared.

Maggie's jaw gaped open and she was speechless.

'You're very kind and you'll be the first to know if we'll be able to take you up on your generous offer,' Chad said softly.

'If young Emily can come to her

senses I have far higher hopes for this one,' Audrey declared, gesturing at Maggie.

She almost asked if anyone had remembered she was there but Chad immediately wrapped his arm around her shoulders making her aware of his calm, reassuring strength all over again.

'So do I,' he murmured. 'Would you consider us rude if we left you now? I'd really enjoy seeing something of St. Ives.'

Maggie was pleased he'd had the courage to ask because she really wanted to show him around. They wouldn't have time to do justice to the Tate Gallery today but he'd get a sense of why the area had drawn thousands of artists over the last hundred and fifty years. She knew in her heart that Chad would join the ranks of its admirers.

'Yes, I would, but you can go anyway. Don't ever waste a moment of the short amount of time you've been given in life. Too many people do,' Audrey said sharply.

Maggie held onto the words, tucking them away to think about later.

18

Chad munched on a hot greasy chip, doused in salt and vinegar by Maggie who'd insisted it was the only way to eat them. He dangled his long legs down over the sea wall and stared out across the inky black sea twinkling with shimmering jewel-bright reflections from the lights strung around the harbour.

They'd walked all around St. Ives, vying with the crowds of tourists packing the narrow streets. Maggie insisted they avoided the gift shops full of Cornish knick-knacks and steered them instead towards the wide array of unique local arts and crafts. He'd bought her a fascinating driftwood figure she'd admired as a memento of the day. Created by a St. Ives artist its flowing hair and enigmatic expression reminded him of Maggie herself.

Eventually the aroma drifting out from the numerous pasty shops stirred his appetite back to life but she'd made him wait until the streets began to empty for a fish and chip supper.

'I'd miss this,' Maggie murmured. 'It's not easy, is it?'

He shook his head and broke off a piece of battered fish, popping it into his mouth and chewing to give himself more thinking time before he replied.

'What's Tennessee like?'

'We have four seasons same as you do except the summers are hotter and more humid. Fall's probably my favourite time of year, the colours are incredible especially up in the Smoky Mountains. We've no coastline of course but there are a ton of beautiful lakes for swimming, boating and fishing.' There was so much more he could say but Chad didn't want Maggie to think he was trying to hard sell her on his home state.

Maggie pinched another of his chips. When they'd placed their order at the shop she'd insisted she didn't want any but had promptly proceeded to eat at least half of his. 'I've never had the opportunity to travel apart from a couple of cheap weekend trips to France.'

'I've been lucky. My folks took us all over the States, plus we did several trips to the Caribbean and two summers we roamed all over Europe. I've done more on my own too. I love seeing how other people live, the differences and the similarities binding us together.' *I want to show you the world, Maggie.* He shoved another chip in his mouth to keep from speaking his undisciplined thoughts out loud.

'Are you close to your family?'

'Yes and no.' Chad shrugged. 'My folks get on at me sometimes for having too active a social life. The way I look at it is I'm single, I'm not in debt and I don't have any addictions beyond the occasional shot of Jack Daniels plus an unhealthy fondness for good fried chicken. Don't get me wrong. I admire their long marriage and that of all my grandparents.' He hesitated over how to express his reservations. 'I don't want to be the one to break the Robertson track record. I guess I'm scared of screwing up.' Maggie frowned and he was afraid he'd been too honest. 'You've made me see it's a cowardly way to live.'

'I have?' She took his last chip out of the paper bag and put it in her mouth, chewing slowly. 'I still can't see how this thing between us is going to work.'

Chad wrapped up the grease-stained paper and set it on the wall next to him before putting his arm back around Maggie.

'Do you remember what Audrey said before we left?' she asked, needing to know if she'd been the only one affected.

'Yep, I sure do, and she's right. Life's too short not to grab it with both hands and make the most of every minute.'

Maggie swallowed the lump forming in her throat, the one she always got thinking about her mother.

'It's the main reason Josh went to live in the wilds of Colorado. My folks wanted him to settle back in Nashville and run the family business. He turned them down flat because he said he'd seen so much ugliness he needed to be surrounded by good, beautiful things for the rest of his life.' Chad pushed a loose strand of Maggie's hair back out of the way and kissed her neck. 'I need to go and see Josh. I let him down badly when he left the army. I should've helped him to stand up to our parents and made them see their way of life wouldn't suit him after what he'd been through.'

'I take it you didn't?'

He shook his head. 'No. I stood back and let them push him until he couldn't take it anymore and left. At the time I didn't try hard enough to understand his motives, but I want to now. You've helped crystallise it in my mind.'

Maggie frowned. 'How?'

'By seeing how you are with Emily.

You never gave up on her no matter how difficult it became. Hey, you haven't been perfect, no one is, but you've always tried.'

She was stunned. No one else had ever understood her complicated relationship with Emily. Chad saw that it wasn't guilt that made her persist with her often difficult sister, it was love.

'Will you come with me to Colorado?' Chad asked, 'I'm not asking for anything beyond your company.' His eyes gleamed in the fading light. 'Of course, I won't object if you choose to share my bed.'

'Oh, won't you?' Maggie said archly, poking him in the ribs.

'I'd love to show you something of my country. You could come to Nashville and meet my folks too, but only if you want to. No pressure. No expectations.'

'Hopes?' she whispered.

'Yeah, I'll definitely have those. I've had them since the moment I set eyes on you, Maggie Taylor.'

The breath left her body and tears prickled at her eyes. She wanted this man so badly her heart ached to think of him leaving.

'Am I way off base?' Chad's soft-spoken question shot directly into her heart and she managed to shake her head. 'Good. How about we head back to Trewarnock now?'

'I suppose we should. Emily might be getting worried,' Maggie said. 'That is if she's even home to notice I'm missing.' She gave him a shy smile. 'Do you know what I'll always remember you saying to me at the wedding?'

Chad kissed her cheek. 'Oh, yeah, I remember. I couldn't imagine anybody not missing you. Still can't, sweetheart.'

'I'll think about your . . . offer. I can't do anything until I've got Emily safely married off.' He went quiet. 'You told me to spit it out earlier, it's your turn now,' she insisted.

'I mentioned hanging around for a few extra days but would it be way out of line for me to suggest staying until after the wedding? I'm owed a ton of vacation days at work so it's not a problem there.'

Maggie guessed it'd taken a lot of courage for him to ask, knowing she could toss the idea right back at him.

'I don't want you to think I'm forcing you to make a decision anytime soon, but . . . I thought you could maybe do with some support.' Chad's uncertainty was at odds with his usual confident manner and somehow that made her feel better.

She wrapped her arms around his neck and kissed him. 'I'd really like that.'

'Really?' He looked so amazed Maggie kissed him again, only this time Chad took the kiss to another level until she forgot everything but him. The hint of salt on his tongue, a rasp of stubble against her cheek, his hard body moulded against hers and his clean, warm scent all took over her senses.

'Oh, Maggie, what am I goin' to do with you?' he murmured, his rapid breaths hot on her skin.

'I'm sure you'll think of something. You usually seem to.' Maggie's voice trembled and she pulled away slightly, unnerved by the powerful effect he had on her. All her usual common sense flew up into the night sky. 'Just love me.' The words tumbled out and a scorching heat lit up her face and neck.

'It's okay,' Chad whispered and trailed a finger down her flaming cheeks. 'I do.'

'But it doesn't make sense.' She tried to be realistic, but the sight of Chad's eyes glittering in the dark fried her brain.

'I know,' he chuckled, 'but did you ever hear anyone call love sensible? It's why so many love songs have the words crazy, reckless and mad in their lyrics.'

'Doesn't it bother you?'

Chad's exuberant laughter rang out and she stared at him.

'It scares the hell out of me but I've never felt so damn good either so I'll take the chance if you will.' He took hold of her hands and Maggie's throat tightened. 'Remember no pressure, no expectations, just hope. I'm good with that for now if you are?'

'Oh, yes.' She made no effort to protest when he pulled her back into his arms and it was a long time before they got around to leaving.

★   ★   ★

Chad called Josh's number and listened to it ring several times. Suddenly his brother's deep, gruff voice answered. 'Hi, it's me. I'm just calling to see how you're doin'.'

'You're over in merry old England schmoozing at some dumb family wedding and you had the wild-assed notion to call me?' Josh's rough laughter hummed down the line. 'Come off it, bro, what's up?'

Be honest. Maggie's compassionate smile filled his vision. 'I needed to tell you I'm sorry. Really sorry.'

'What for?'

'Being a lousy brother. Not helping when you needed it. Everything I guess,' Chad admitted, exhaling a long slow breath when he'd finished.

'What's brought this on?' Josh was always direct and no-nonsense. He'd been that way before he joined the military and it'd solidified his natural inclinations. 'Don't get me wrong. I appreciate it,' his voice wavered, 'but why now?'

'I've been thinkin' okay?' That wasn't good enough. 'I met someone . . . '

Josh chuckled. 'Who is she?'

'How do you know it's a woman?'

'Always is, unless you're the other way inclined and I'm pretty sure that's not the case where you're concerned,' Josh stated bluntly. 'I've seen it a million times.'

'You too?' A heavy silence hummed along the phone line.

'Yeah.' Josh exhaled a deep sigh. 'I'll tell you about it one day. It didn't work out.'

He didn't push and quickly changed the subject. 'You didn't reply to my email but I'm guessin' it's okay for me to come visit? I might bring someone with me.'

'Sure. Anytime. I'd enjoy meeting the lucky lady too.'

Chad began to tell him about Maggie and found he couldn't stop, needing Josh to understand how special she was to him.

'Okay, I get it,' Josh laughed, 'she's beautiful, intelligent, sexy, can cook and for some wacky reason thinks you're the greatest thing since sliced bread. The woman obviously doesn't have an atom of sense,' he teased.

'Thanks. Now I remember why I've missed having you around,' Chad joked, but his voice broke. 'I'd better go. Things to do.' He needed to get off the phone before making a complete fool of himself. After he disconnected Chad laid back on the bed, smiling and biting back tears.

19

Maggie plastered on another bright smile. It'd taken every ounce of self-control to get through the last ten days and if it hadn't been for Chad she suspected she'd have been carted off in a straitjacket. For someone who'd declared she wanted a simple wedding Emily was being very picky. Six more days — that was all she had to get through.

'You *promised* you'd come with me for the fitting,' Emily wailed, 'I know the dress is going to be too tight. My stomach is *enormous*.'

She glanced over at her sister and sighed. Even at four months pregnant she was still sylph-like compared to Maggie and barely showing at all. They'd returned the extravagant white tulle ball-gown Emily originally chose and replaced it with an elegant knee-length champagne silk dress.

'I can come if you change the time to four o'clock but I have to be here at two because that's when the shrimp and scallops are being delivered.'

'Sorry for butting in,' Chad interrupted, 'but I could fish sit if necessary. I'm guessin' I can recognise a decent shrimp when I see one.'

Maggie hated taking advantage of him again — the poor man had been run ragged between doing things for her and cheerfully running errands for Emily. She'd insisted on him taking a few sightseeing trips, but he'd refused most of her suggestions saying he'd rather be with her. He did track down an antiques shop in Redruth specialising in all things Art Deco. It'd been recommended by Audrey and he'd immediately rushed off afterwards to show her godmother everything he'd bought. They'd struck up a curious friendship consisting of a lot of good-natured bickering mixed with a deep mutual respect.

'You're an angel.' Emily flung herself at Chad and gave him a big hug. 'If I wasn't marrying my wonderful Jonathan I'd snatch you up myself.'

'I'll take care of your fish on one condition.' Chad explained. 'In return your sister gets the next twenty-four hours off.'

Before Maggie could protest Emily happily agreed.

'But there's so much to do, I can't possibly . . . '

'Yes, you can,' Emily insisted. 'I've been taking advantage of your good nature. I can do more myself with Jonathan's help and the other stuff can wait a couple of days.'

This wasn't the first time her sister had been thoughtful and she needed to acknowledge the fact. All brides were picky — it came with the territory and Emily wasn't behaving any worse than the other girls she'd designed cakes for who'd made her want to throw up her hands in despair.

'Thanks, Ems.' If she said any more

she'd cry. Maggie watched her sister's eyes mist up and knew they were on the same shaky emotional page.

'I'm going to take a nap before lunch. It's one of the few perks of pregnancy. I'll leave you two to do whatever.' Emily laughed and breezed out of the room.

'So kid, you fancy some . . . whatever?'

Chad's raised eyebrows and quirky smile made Maggie relax for the first time in days. He held out his hand and she quickly went over to him and snuggled into his lap.

'Do you have plans for our mini-holiday?' Maggie asked and a wicked smile accentuated his handsome features. 'Apart from . . . you know, the obvious.'

He kissed all the way down her neck, stopping only when her clothes got in the way. 'And what might 'the obvious' be, honey?'

'Stop cross-examining me,' she half-heartedly protested, sighing as he slipped one hand under the hem of her blouse and stroked her bare skin, heating it on contact.

'Guilty as charged.' Chad's fingers carried on their searing explorations. 'Your wonderful Great Aunt Audrey has gone to visit some poor cousin in Wales and she's offered us the hospitality of Holland House for the night.'

Maggie stared in disbelief. 'You're joking?'

'Nope.'

'But we're not married and she's really strict about, you know,' she mumbled.

'Is 'you know' the same as 'the obvious'?' Before she could answer he kissed her again making her head swim. 'I've been informed there are two guest bedrooms available for our use. Audrey gave me a very arched look and said that as we were both over the age of majority what we did with them was up to us.'

'I dread to imagine how you replied.' Maggie shuddered, certain he'd been his usual outspoken self.

'I didn't. I merely gave her an equally snooty look in return and tapped my finger against my nose politely, making it clear she needed to mind her own business.' Chad's warm laughter rumbled through her. 'So, are you up for an adventure tonight?'

The old Maggie would've thought about it, weighed the pros and cons and come down on the side of caution but the chance of spending the next twenty-four hours being loved and fussed over was too enticing to turn down.

'Good.' He hugged her.

'But I haven't answered yet,' Maggie protested.

'You don't need to. I watched you decide and your eyes went all soft and misty.'

'Could you possibly sound any more self-satisfied?' She tried to pull away but he wouldn't loosen his hold.

Chad smirked. 'Oh, I could, but then you might damage me irreparably and neither of us would have any fun tonight.' He brushed a lock of hair out of his eyes and went back to nuzzling her neck, murmuring how good she tasted before going into explicit details about what he planned to do to her later. Listening to him heated her blood. 'Why don't you go and get packed so we can escape as soon as you're done with the Demon Bride? You won't need much. You won't be going far.'

For a few brief moments Maggie wondered what on earth she thought she was doing.

'Hey, don't fret, I'm only having a bit of fun with you. There's nothing wrong with us enjoying being together, Maggie, in whatever way we choose. The crucial word is *choose*, honey.'

She let out the smile she'd been fighting. 'In that case I *choose* to go with you and I *choose* to have a good time.'

'You're an amazing woman, Maggie Taylor.'

You're pretty amazing too. She'd tell him that later, when the time was right.

* * *

Maggie had said several times how much she admired his innate confidence, but there was a fine line between that and arrogance, something he never wanted to be with her or anyone else. She had the crazy idea it'd been a tough week for him but didn't appear to realise how much he'd enjoyed being a part of her life. It didn't matter if he'd been emptying the trash or running Emily to a whole raft of shoe shops while Maggie was busy making the wedding cake.

Tonight he'd try his best to tell her.

'You'd better go now and do whatever you need to do. I'll fix myself a cup of coffee while I wait.' He shooed her out of the kitchen. With the kettle turned on Chad found a mug and a jar of instant coffee. He opened a drawer in his search for a spoon. The next one he tried was one of the catch-all variety everyone had in their house and before he could close it back up a crumpled photo stuck in the back corner caught his eye. Chad couldn't resist pulling it out.

A smiling woman with Maggie's brown wavy hair but Emily's tall, slender build stared back at him. She was crouching down on the grass with her arms wrapped around two little girls in matching blue dresses.

'Our mother was an incredibly special person.' Emily's soft voice startled him and he turned to stare at her, standing in the kitchen doorway with her eyes full of tears. 'Did Maggie tell you about her?'

He couldn't lie. 'Only a little.'

Emily's trembling hands smoothed down the front of her yellow sundress. 'I'm sure she mentioned how our mother died.'

'Yeah, she did.'

'I blamed her for the longest time.'

'And she let you. So did your father.' Chad murmured. 'It wasn't fair.'

'I realise that now. Our father should've stood up for her but he didn't.'

'Because your behaviour made it impossible for him to do so.' Maggie would hate him if he made things worse but he needed to be truthful.

'You don't pull any punches, do you?' Emily half smiled. 'Jonathan doesn't either these days and that's good for me. No one ever did that before. They let me get away with being thoughtless and badly behaved.'

Chad nodded. 'Do you know the best gift you could give Maggie?'

'My head on a platter?' she teased.

'Nothing as extreme. A genuine apology would do.' Her eyes narrowed and he worried he'd gone too far. Emily needed to know he wasn't firing a shot in the dark. 'I called my brother last week and did the same thing. He's a lot older and we've never been close. I wasn't there when he needed my support and I want things to be different between us. Maggie helped me get it straight in my head.'

'Maybe I'm not as brave as you,' Emily ventured.

'You can be as brave as you want to be. Think about it while we're away tonight.'

She gave him a long, piercing stare before turning around and walking back upstairs.

Chad wasn't sure if he'd opened his big, fat mouth, stuck his size twelve feet in there and stomped around. Any second now Maggie could fly through the door furious at him for upsetting her sister. He went back to making his coffee and kept his fingers crossed.

20

'You sure you're okay with the fish thing?' Maggie breezed into the kitchen.

'Yeah, of course I am.'

She caught a touch of relief in Chad's voice but didn't make any comment. 'Hopefully we won't be too long, but who knows?'

'Take as long as you need.' Chad reassured her. 'Is your sister ready to go?'

'I certainly am.' Emily appeared in the doorway. Her brisk reply appeared to startle Chad judging by the sudden flash of heat colouring his face and neck.

'What's up with you two?' Maggie demanded. 'If it's a nice secret you can keep it, otherwise I want to know.'

'I'd say it's good, wouldn't you, Emily?' Chad's tight smile didn't reach his eyes.

'Hopefully.' Emily grabbed Maggie's arm. 'Come on or we'll be late.'

'But . . . '

'Later, honey.' Chad fixed his gaze on her. She got the hint that he needed her to let it go for now, but it didn't mean she had to like it. Maggie went over and bent down to kiss him.

'I'll hold you to that,' she whispered before swinging back around to give Emily a broad smile. 'Let's go.'

★   ★   ★

On the drive home Emily laid back in the seat and closed her eyes but Maggie wasn't convinced her sister was sleeping. They'd had a good time at the bridal shop and hadn't spoken about anything more serious than what flowers Emily wanted in her hair on the wedding day, replacing the original tiara and lace veil she'd planned. Her sister's fears about the new dress had been unfounded and Maggie had fought back tears at seeing Emily looking so radiant.

She noticed dark shadows under her sister's eyes and decided not to spoil the day with difficult questions.

'I'm sorry, Maggie.'

'What for?' A multitude of things raced through her mind, none of them good. Slow tears trickled down Emily's cheeks and Maggie couldn't keep on driving. She quickly pulled off the road to stop outside the hairdresser's shop. Maggie remembered the guilty look lurking in Chad's eyes earlier and she clutched the steering wheel. 'Did Chad say something to you?' The words barely made their way past her lips.

'In a way,' Emily admitted.

'I suppose he told you everything I confessed to him about Mum's death?' How could he? She'd trusted Chad with her deepest feelings and now he'd made a mockery of them. It was up to her when and where she tackled Emily, not him.

Emily frowned. 'What on earth are you talking about?' She quietly explained everything that went on in the kitchen and the challenge he'd given her to put things right with Maggie.

Relief coursed through her blood and Maggie could've wept with happiness. 'I'm sorry. I was stupid, I . . . '

'It's okay,' Emily reassured. 'It makes a change for you to be the impulsive one. It's usually me flying off the handle and zooming off into drama queen land.'

'So, what *are* you sorry for?'

'How about the way I've behaved towards you since the day you were born? Will that do for a start? I resented your arrival because it took Mum and Dad's attention away from me. I'm especially sorry for the way I've been such a cow since Mum died. What happened to her was an accident and it wasn't ever your fault.'

Maggie's head spun. Her emotions veered from being cross at Chad for interfering and wanting to kiss him senseless for being so flagrantly on her side.

'Your man was absolutely right. Of course I didn't want to see it at first but when he explained how he'd made things right with his own brother at your insistence I completely understood where he was coming from.'

Maggie had no idea what Emily was talking about. Putting the pieces together she guessed Chad's talk with Josh must've happened last week. They'd had so little time alone he obviously hadn't found the right moment to tell her yet.

'Will you ever be able to forgive me?' Emily begged.

'Of course, you daft creature.'

'Really? I don't promise to be perfect.'

'Thank goodness for that,' Maggie laughed. 'I want my own sister, not some fake version I wouldn't recognise.'

Emily's expression turned serious. 'This is the perfect time for a fresh start isn't it?'

'It certainly is,' Maggie agreed, too choked up to say anymore. 'Now how about we get you home so you can get pretty for Jonathan, and . . . '

'You can get ready for your dirty night out.'

'It's not going to be like that,' she protested. Emily's raucous laughter silenced her. Maggie started the car back up and had to ignore Emily's sniggers all the way home.

★   ★   ★

Chad checked his watch as he stopped outside Maggie's house. She'd told him to come back at six to pick her up. The two sisters were laughing and joking when they returned from their outing which could simply mean the dress fitting went well but with any luck Emily had already apologised. One way or the other Maggie would tackle him about it as soon as they were alone. She wasn't a woman to put things off.

He strolled up the path and the door opened before he could knock. Emily grabbed his arm and pulled him inside.

'She's nearly ready.'

'I *am* ready. Some of us prefer to be punctual.' Maggie's voice next to him made Chad turn around.

He'd no idea what she'd done to herself, but the breath left his body. Chad smelled her familiar vanilla scent but everything else was an amped up version of his beautiful Maggie. Everything about her glowed, from the gleaming waves of rich brown hair grazing her bare creamy shoulders to the dusty peach gloss on her full mouth and her eyes. He could barely resist the urge to touch her.

'Do you like Maggie's new dress? You can't imagine how hard it was for me to get her to shop for herself today,' Emily prattled.

'It's stunning,' he murmured. By the parts he *could* see Chad knew she was hot all over. The simple bronze silk dress skimmed her luscious curves, with the low-scooped neckline dropping delicious hints about her generous cleavage and the hemline barely grazing her knees showed off her shapely legs.

'I've made her throw away the awful green thing she's worn to every wedding since the beginning of creation,' Emily boasted.

Thank goodness. If Emily hadn't done the deed he'd planned to take a pair of scissors to it at the first opportunity.

'You just wait until you see her bridesmaid's dress.' Emily grinned.

'Please tell me it's not one of those awful puffy things in a putrid colour designed not to outshine the bride,' he joked.

'I promise it'll put Pippa Middleton's in the shade.'

He'd no idea what she was talking about. 'I'm damn sure it will.' *Because it'll have this gorgeous woman wearing it.*

Maggie loudly cleared her throat. 'Excuse me. I am here in case you've forgotten.'

I couldn't forget you in a million years and I'll prove it to you if I can get you out of here. 'If you're ready we can leave.' *Please put me out of my misery.*

'Oh, I'm ready,' she focused her dark blue eyes solely on him and Chad swallowed hard. He held out his hand and she placed her soft, warm fingers in his palm.

The next half-hour was a blur as he drove them to Holland House. They spoke very little and Chad guessed she'd realised he couldn't concentrate on both the road and her. Finally inside the house he shut Audrey's apartment door behind them and exhaled slowly.

At last he could touch her properly. Chad clasped his arms around her waist and breathed in her heady fragrance. 'I know you want to talk,' he murmured against the soft skin of her neck. 'But . . .'

'Later,' she pleaded, 'we've got all night and right now I want you so badly it hurts.'

'Where does it hurt?' Chad's voice roughened.

'Right here.' She took his hand and

placed it over her fast-beating heart. He stroked his fingers over the slippery fabric and captured her soft moans with his mouth.

'I know the cure.'

'I thought you might.' Maggie sighed and arched into his touch.

Chad slid his other hand around her back and began to work her zip down, inch by inch. She begged him to hurry but he only smiled. 'Patience, Maggie, patience.' His own hung by a thread but he tried not to show it.

'Could we be patient next time, please?' Her eyelashes fluttered temptingly as he reached the base of her spine.

'Next time? You're thinking of more than once?' Chad cupped her backside and eased her closer, allowing her to rub up against him and swiftly drive him insane.

She whispered in his ear, telling him exactly what she wanted him to do and her low, sexy laughter made every cell in his body stand to attention.

'A well brought up Southern gentleman always tries to please a lady.' Chad pushed her dress down over her shoulders and eased it slowly past her hips, letting it drop to the floor in a pool of gleaming satin. 'We'll take this into the bedroom.'

'That's the best idea I've heard all week.' Maggie's eyes shone. 'Love me.'

'Yes, ma'am.' For the next few precious hours he intended to make her feel so loved and cherished she wouldn't be able to imagine her life without him. He only hoped he was up to the challenge.

21

'Breakfast?' Chad murmured, lifting a handful of hair from her neck and pressing warm kisses into her sensitive skin.

'Are you offering yourself on toast?' Maggie teased, wriggling around to face him. She still found it hard to grasp the idea that this seriously gorgeous man was attracted to *her*. But it wasn't simply his looks, although she could happily gaze at him for hours and did so last night when she was too wired to sleep. He was intelligent, witty and caring — and Maggie couldn't imagine what she'd done to be so fortunate.

'I'm offerin' myself in any way you want me, sweetheart.' Chad's smooth drawl made her heart race and his large, sure hands cupped her hips, hitching them closer making her aware of every rock-hard inch of his body.

'I'm versatile, like an egg.' His rumbling chuckle ran right through her blood. 'You've scrambled my brain, fried my common sense and boiled all my gentlemanly intentions away. There's not much left to try.'

Maggie insinuated her hands up through his hair, playing with the heavy, dark strands and breathing in his delicious musky scent. 'Poaching is a good method that leaves the outside firm and the inside gooey and delectable.'

He groaned and seized her in a fierce kiss, rolling them over until he was on top. 'That's enough game playing, Miss Taylor. Time for action.'

Maggie's last attempt at coherent thought faded away as he slid deep inside her with a satisfied groan, making her his all over again.

Afterwards she drifted back to sleep until bright light flooded the room and woke her up.

'Here's breakfast in bed for the sexiest cake decorator ever.'

Maggie opened her eyes and focused on Chad, posing in front of her in only a pair of black boxers and brandishing a large silver tray. 'Slept with a lot of them have you?'

He didn't reply, just settled the tray over her knees and walked around to sit down next to her on the bed. Chad poured her tea exactly the way she liked it and lifted the cover off the plate to reveal two perfectly poached eggs on wheat toast.

'Eat up while they're still fresh,' he said softly.

She hadn't meant to hurt his feelings and should know by now he was sensitive about his perceived reputation with women. Maggie forced down a forkful of eggs. 'These aren't easy to make. You never told me you could cook.'

'There's a lot you don't know about me, Maggie.' Chad's tawny eyes bored right through her.

'Maybe it's time you told me . . . before we go any further.' She pushed away the tray, her appetite gone.

* * *

Chad watched the light leave her beautiful face. She'd been so happy and now he'd spoiled everything. 'You know a lot of it already.'

'Then why be so serious?'

Chad risked putting his arms around her. He buried his face in her hair and smelled the fragrant hints of vanilla in her silky curls.

'You've forced me to be more honest.' He needed to get this over with. 'I want to tell you first what my grandmother said before I came over here. She's very much like Audrey, a plain spoken woman who gives advice whether you want it or not.' Chad recited word for word everything she'd said and watched Maggie's eyes widen.

Use this vacation as a chance to take some time out, Chandler. Playing the field is all very well for a young man, but you're old enough to start thinking more about the future. Your father won't come out and say so but I know he'd like to take things easier. He's been hoping you'd decide to give up the law and take over the firm. Josh needs our help as well but he's too stubborn to ask for it. You could do a lot for him if you chose to.

'I know I'm not the first girl you've taken to bed, I'm not stupid, Chad.'

'I never said you were.' It pained him to hear the unvarnished hurt in Maggie's voice. 'I need you to believe me when I say it's different with you. I've been called glib and silver-tongued but I swear to you I've never deliberately misled any woman about how I felt.' His impassioned plea got no response beyond a simple nod. 'Say something. Please. You're killing me.'

A tiny smile tugged at her lips. 'I'd hoped you knew me better than this.'

He wasn't sure how to reply so kept his mouth shut.

'If I thought for one moment I was

simply another notch on your bedpost I wouldn't be here,' Maggie assured him and the tense knots in his stomach unravelled.

Chad managed to breathe properly again. 'God, Maggie, I love you so much.'

She gazed up at him, her blue eyes swimming with tears. 'I love you too, you silly man. You freaked me out. I was afraid you were going to tell me something awful. Now I want to hear all about your brother and this family business you've never mentioned.' The sharper edge to her voice told Chad he was forgiven but if he didn't spit out all the rest of it he'd be toast — with or without the famous poached eggs.

'Have you heard of Robertson guitars?' He ventured.

'Of course I have, my father used to own one.' Maggie's countenance changed. 'That's *you*?'

Chad shrugged. 'Well, yeah, I guess it is.'

'It either is or it isn't.'

'Okay then, it is.' He sighed. 'My full name is Chandler Winston Robertson the fourth. My great-grandfather, Joshua Robertson, started the business in 1920 with his younger brother, Chandler, and it became a big success. We make some of the most sought after guitars in the world. The eldest son has always become the company president but Josh isn't interested in taking over after my father.' Chad's voice faltered and Maggie squeezed his hand 'There were fierce arguments when Josh declared his intention to join the military. I was only eight when Josh left home but I heard it all. Because of my parents' attitude Josh basically cut himself off from the family.' The memories of being angry at his older brother for leaving all flooded back and Chad tried to explain to Maggie how it'd made him more stubborn. He'd refused to join the business too and had gone to law school instead. 'Not because I wasn't interested in guitar making, I loved it when I worked there in the school vacations, but out of sheer bull-headed stubbornness.'

'You idiot.'

'Thanks a lot,' he grumbled. 'Yeah, yeah, alright, I know I'm a moron. I don't hate my job but it's not my real passion.' He needed to explain more about Josh. 'When my brother came back unscathed from Afghanistan, at least physically, my parents wanted to take care of him but he rejected all their offers. I didn't stand up for him and I should've done. None of us tried to understand that it was beyond Josh to fit back into the mould that had been made for him.'

'We all have to make our own moulds, don't we?'

'You don't fit into Emily's catering one either do you?'

'Nope,' Maggie declared with a laugh. 'Cakes I love, Scotch eggs you can . . .'

'Turn into ammunition as far as I'm concerned. No offence to Emily.' Chad shuddered.

'So, you're going into the guitar business?'

Until now he'd only ever admitted it in his head but he couldn't lie to Maggie. 'You wouldn't mind?' She shook her head. Wisely she didn't ask him to spell it out any clearer. 'I called Josh last week and apologised. That's what I talked to Emily about. I wanted her to understand how important it was for her to reach out to you. I'd intended to tell you first, honestly.'

'I get it. I'm not cross at you. Life's been so crazy we haven't had a minute on our own.'

'Tell me about it,' he said with a wry smile. 'I'll still feel better once I make my peace with Josh face to face.' Chad eased Maggie over onto his lap, there was nothing better than having his arms full of soft, beautiful woman. 'They'll all love you.' She flashed a glorious smile.

'I hope so.'

'I *know* so.' Chad glanced at the

abandoned tray. 'I'm sorry I spoiled your breakfast.'

Maggie wrapped her arms around his neck and drew him to her for a long, deep kiss. 'Do I seem a disappointed woman?'

'I'm not sure.' He frowned, pretending to be uncertain. 'Maybe another kiss would convince me?'

She took him at his word and the cold poached eggs were forgotten . . . again.

* * *

'You'd prefer to go back home before the twenty-four limit is up, wouldn't you?' Chad's voice from somewhere behind her shoulder startled Maggie. She'd sneaked out of bed while he was still asleep to make a cup of tea.

How did he know her so well already? She couldn't stop thinking about all the things on her to-do list.

'You won't relax and enjoy the rest of the day if I keep you here.' He turned her around to face him. 'It's okay. I'll let you off.'

She tried not to be distracted by the fact he hadn't bothered to get dressed before coming to look for her. It was a challenge to keep her mind on vol-au-vents and fruit cake while plastered up against six feet of naked, gorgeous man. By his wide grin she knew he'd read her mind.

'Don't worry, honey, I *know* what you'd rather be doing, but your conscience is a very active creature and we'll enjoy each other more when your mind isn't elsewhere.' He squeezed her tighter and Maggie squealed. 'I'm goin' to shower and get dressed. You can fix me a cup of coffee if that isn't too much trouble and then we'll head back to face Bridezilla.'

Maggie couldn't resist another kiss but it used every atom of self-restraint she possessed to stop there. 'You are one very special man.'

'Keep believin' that and we'll be good,' Chad teased and let her go. He sauntered out of the kitchen, giving a quick shimmy of his hips to make it abundantly clear what she was missing out on.

She groaned and heard him chuckle as he headed off towards the bedroom.

22

'Ready for Round Two?' Maggie's cheery voice made Chad look up from the tables he'd been arranging. 'I bet you didn't think you'd be back at Polvennor House again?'

That was the understatement of the century. 'You could say that. How's our dear Emily this morning?'

Maggie laughed. 'About as calm as you'd expect a hormonal, overwrought woman to be. Thankfully Aunt Judy is holding her hand while we get the last details finished for the reception.' She glanced around with satisfaction. 'I still can't believe we were lucky enough to get an opening here at the last minute.'

'It's a neat place,' Chad agreed and held out his arms to Maggie. 'You look like a woman in need of serious kissing.'

'And why would you say that?' The question was at odds with the way she hurried to nestle against him, making happy sighs as he stroked his hands up and down her spine. When she fixed her deep blue eyes on him and slowly trailed her tongue around his mouth Maggie drove him nearly out of his mind.

'You little minx,' he half-heartedly complained.

'We need to get the cake in from the car.'

'Yeah, cake, will do.' Chad murmured and went back to kissing her.

'Um, I'm afraid it has to be now.' Maggie wriggled out of his embrace and frowned at her watch. 'We've got twenty minutes to finish up and get back to the house.'

'Slave driver,' Chad groused. She didn't take him seriously and popped a quick kiss on his forehead before flitting back to the kitchen. He followed along behind, exactly as he'd done that first day and didn't make any attempt to wipe the smile from his face.

*   *   *

Maggie hadn't expected to find Emily's wedding day so emotional and without Chad's steady presence would have spent it as a blubbering wreck. As it was she'd held out until one o'clock when Emily walked down the stairs ready to leave for the wedding before dissolving into tears. The champagne silk dress made her sister's skin glow and the circle of creamy roses nestled in her blonde hair were the perfect final touch. 'Oh, Ems, you look so beautiful. I wish Mum and Dad were here to see you.'

'Me too.' Emily held Maggie's hands. 'But I've got you and I'm so grateful for that.'

'The car's here if you're both ready,' Chad said, strolling in from outside. 'I'm a lucky guy to have two lovely ladies to admire.'

'You certainly are. Make sure you appreciate it,' Maggie joked.

His eyes darkened as he checked her out. 'Oh, I do, honey. No question about it.' Chad fingered the stiff taffeta of her dress. 'Where did you find this? It's gorgeous.'

Maggie lowered her gaze to the floor under his intense scrutiny. 'Emily and I sneaked off last week to your favourite shop in Redruth. The lady was most helpful when we mentioned your name, probably because you made all her business dreams come true when you spent the equivalent of a small country's gross national income there.'

'She had some good stuff,' Chad explained unapologetically.

'I told her I was interested in something vintage but not a straight up and down flapper dresses because it wouldn't suit my figure. She told me this was a tea gown from 1930.' Maggie loved the way it draped around her curves, falling barely to her ankles, and making her feel pretty and feminine. The cream background and small pale gold pattern was a perfect foil for Emily's wedding dress.

'You could at least *pretend* I'm the

most beautiful, after all it is my wedding day,' Emily pretended to be offended.

'You are definitely the most beautiful bride, and Maggie's the most beautiful bridesmaid. How's that? Everyone happy now?'

'I certainly am.' Maggie linked her arm with his. 'I'm pretty sure my annoying sister is too. Let's go and get her married.' She opened the front door and let her Aunt Judy and Emily walk out first. They got into the cream Rolls-Royce trimmed with fluttering silk ribbons. Chad was driving them in his rental car so they could get away quickly after the ceremony. She wanted to make sure everything was ready at the reception before her staff took over. Maggie knew she wouldn't enjoy herself if she didn't make sure there'd be no repeat of the mutilated cake incident.

Out in the car Chad didn't start the engine straight away but stared at her again, touching her face so gently her heart flooded with love for him. He wore the same suit he'd had for Fiona's wedding and the memories slammed back, only a few weeks on the calendar but so much more in her head. He'd looked handsome then but today everything was quite different. Maggie knew about the scar on his knee from a bad fall on the basketball court, the odd way his middle left toe was longer than any of the others and his new craving for English chips with salt and plenty of vinegar.

'Does it seem quite as crazy now?' he whispered. 'I've jumped off the cliff, you goin' to join me?'

'What're you asking?'

'Come with me to Colorado next week.'

'Would we go to Nashville as well while we're there?'

He brushed his lips across hers, barely a kiss but sending a waft of citrusy cologne her way. 'Only if you want.'

Maggie nodded and Chad's contented smile brought tears flooding back to her eyes. She blinked really hard, determined not to spoil the make-up Emily had spent far too long applying earlier.

Nothing more needed to be said, not now. He turned the key in the ignition and whistled the Wedding March as he pulled out from the kerb.

★ ★ ★

Chad had never been as uncomplicatedly happy in his life and wanted to savour every moment. Weddings didn't usually get to him emotionally but today's did. Maybe it was seeing Emily and Jonathan so sure of each other now, their eyes never leaving each other's faces as they said their vows but Chad decided it had more to do with the woman tucked into his side. She fitted there as if she'd been made for him and his fanciful side thought she probably had been.

He'd felt his grandmother's satisfied smile over the phone when he'd called to say he might bring someone to meet her soon. Of course he'd got her standard interrogation but must have answered in a satisfactory manner because she ended the conversation by ordering him not to wait too long because she didn't have long to live. She'd been threatening the family with her imminent demise as long as he could remember and, although she was nearly ninety, it still seemed a far off possibility.

Maggie brushed away a tear from his cheek. 'You big old softie. I'm supposed to be the one crying.'

'I got something in my eye, that's all,' he muttered.

'Right. Come on. Let's follow them out. We'll hang around for a couple of photos and then make our escape,' Maggie ordered. Chad wished they could run off on their own now. It'd been beyond cruel of her to describe her new cream lace underwear when they were on their way to the wedding. He could only thank the Lord it was an afternoon wedding and by four o'clock the happy couple would be on the train from Truro, off to enjoy a brief honeymoon in London.

Soon they were back at Polzennor House where it'd all begun. They held hands as they walked into the entrance hall, automatically stopping at the door into the reception room.

'No seating plan today?'

Maggie gave him a sly smile. 'It isn't necessary with twenty guests.'

'So I'm not going to be stuck on the Reject Table with a bunch of losers?'

She poked his ribs. 'No. You get the privilege of sitting next to the second most beautiful woman here today.'

'Why do I get cheated out of the number one hottie?'

'Because her new husband would hit you if you make a move on her.'

Chad fake-sighed. 'I guess I'll have to put up with you then.'

'If you're not careful I might sit by Jonathan's brother. I hear he's got an extensive toy train collection.'

'Maybe we'll land him with Tonya at . . . ' Chad bit his tongue. He'd almost cracked a joke about their own wedding but she might not find the idea funny — yet. 'I just meant whoever gets married next. Um, they could . . . ' His throat closed up and he stared down at the floor.

'Let's sneak a glass of champagne before everyone else arrives.' Maggie took a firm grasp of his hand. 'We should drink a toast to Reject Tables everywhere.'

'Absolutely.' He kissed her, tasting the sweetness that was uniquely his Maggie. 'For some reason I've suddenly become a big fan.'

We do hope that you have enjoyed reading this large print book.

Did you know that all of our titles are available for purchase?

We publish a wide range of high quality large print books including:
Romances, Mysteries, Classics
General Fiction
Non Fiction and Westerns

Special interest titles available in large print are:
The Little Oxford Dictionary
Music Book, Song Book
Hymn Book, Service Book

Also available from us courtesy of Oxford University Press:
Young Readers' Dictionary
(large print edition)
Young Readers' Thesaurus
(large print edition)

For further information or a free brochure, please contact us at:
Ulverscroft Large Print Books Ltd.,
The Green, Bradgate Road, Anstey,
Leicester, LE7 7FU, England.
Tel: (00 44) **0116 236 4325**
Fax: (00 44) **0116 234 0205**

HOLLY'S CHRISTMAS KISS

Alison May

Holly Michelle Jolly hates Christmas, and she has good reason to. Apart from her ridiculously festive name, tragic and unfortunate events have a habit of happening to her around the holiday season. And this year is no different. After the flight to her once-in-a-lifetime holiday destination is cancelled, she faces the prospect of a cold and lonely Christmas. That is, until she meets Sean Munro. With Sean's help, can she experience her first happy Christmas, or will their meeting just result in more memories she'd rather forget?

LOVE ON TRACK

Jill Barry

Flora Petersen surprises family and friends when she successfully applies for a job as a train manager. Though nervous to begin with, she soon finds herself enjoying the daily routine of assisting passengers — including one she privately nick-names 'Mr Gorgeous'. Jack, father of a small daughter, commutes to his job via train. Since his wife died, he's had no time for romance. Until one day he notices the lovely woman who sells him a ticket, and realises he's seen her somewhere before . . .

ISLAND MAGIC

Margaret Mounsdon

Vanessa Blake's sister asks her to take her place as dance professional on a private yacht owned by the Petucci family — then promptly disappears. When a priceless ring goes missing on the yacht, Vanessa realises she is high on the list of suspects. Taking refuge on the island of Santa Agathe, she thinks she is safe — until a valuable painting by local artist Severino, with whom she is staying, is stolen. Can Vanessa trust security chief Lorenzo Talbot to help prove her innocence, or does he have his own agenda?

HOPE FOR HANNAH

Linda Mitchelmore

Hannah French has always wanted more from life than her sleepy Dartmoor village can offer. On the wild moors, she loses herself in poetry and dreams of escape. Two brothers are eager to help: gentle, kind and sensitive William, a painter who yearns for a creative life in France or Italy; and rugged, dangerous and extravagant Ralph, who is equally keen to show Hannah the world outside Dartmoor — but at what cost? When events in Hannah's life take a devastating turn, she is no longer certain who she can trust . . .

I'LL ALWAYS BE THERE

Susan Udy

When Becca is persuaded to attend a speed-dating evening, she has no notion of the chain of events it will set in motion. She meets three men: Marco, Gary and Andy. Marco introduces her to wealthy entrepreneur Lando Wheatley, who turns out to be the landlord of the beauty salon she runs with her friend Lizzie. Then there's Sam, Lizzie's brother, who she once dated. When someone begins to stalk her, Becca doesn't know which of the men she can trust, and which might have an out-of-control possessive streak . . .

WOMAN OF MYSTERY

Ken Preston

While on a study holiday in Italy, researching the mysterious last paintings of Lorenzo Gagliardi, Jessica Matthews is advised to search out Noah Glassman, a visiting lecturer at the local university, for help. To her frustration, she finds him both abrasive and attractive. Events take a sinister turn when Noah's office is vandalised — and then a Gagliardi painting is damaged in a break-in at an exhibition. Who could have a motive for the crimes — and what secrets are waiting to be discovered within the ancient monastic foundations of the university?